I0624477

THEY DO EXIST!

Anthology of Award-winning Short Stories

Copyright ©2006 by Scribes Valley Publishing Company. All rights reserved. Individual authors in this anthology retain copyright to their material and all rights revert to them. No part of this publication may be reproduced, stored in a retrieval system or transmitted in any form or by any means electronic, mechanical, photocopying, recording, or otherwise, except in the case of brief quotations embodied in critical articles or reviews, without the prior written permission of the publisher and individual author.

The stories in this anthology are works of fiction. Characters, names, places, and incidents are products of the authors' imagination or are used fictitiously.

ISBN-13: 978-0-9742652-4-7
ISBN-10: 0-9742652-4-1

DEDICATION

This anthology is dedicated to those who know
great stories *do* exist.

To the authors featured in this book: Scribes Valley thanks you for
your time, patience, trust, and talent.

TABLE OF CONTENTS

THEY DO EXIST!
A Foreword by David L. Repsher, editor

How many times have you heard someone say there's nothing good to read? Unfortunately, I hear it way too often from know-it-alls who are sure all the great stories have gone the way of the dinosaurs. And that sends shivers down my back.

Nothing good to read. Good grief, is there a more depressing phrase than that? Well, I guess there is. Like, "The dog just ate my last pair of underwear" or "Didn't you notice the horrible fungus growing on that last piece of pepperoni before you ate it?" But, I'm just talking about reading right now.

Sure, the world is filled with stories that never quite achieve "great" status. How sad it is for someone willing to take precious time, to sit down to read, and get...nothing. Nothing, except that horrible empty feeling of an unfulfilled imagination, of expectations dropping like a brick in a pond, of feelings dragged through the muck and mire of a story that just isn't there.

Okay, maybe it's not *that* bad, but you have to admit, reading a story that just doesn't do it for you can be a bit disheartening.

Trust me, you won't find any of those in this anthology!

Now, what makes a great story? Glad you asked. A great story grabs you by the throat and won't let go, taking you away from the everyday world and giving you new worlds to explore, new situations to experience, and the incredible feeling of being better for having gone.

Think back to all the stories you've read in your life. Now, write all the titles down on a sheet of paper along with the author's name and number of pages and.... Just kidding. Try to remember the thrill you felt as a story made your pulse pound, your breath quicken, your fingers fly as they turned the pages. Try to remember the far-off places you visited and the adventures you had while never leaving your seat.

Think those memories and feelings are gone forever? Wrong. Great stories are out there, waiting to be discovered and cherished, waiting to take up occupancy in your mind, to remind you again and again that you can leave the real world with all its troubles and worries and cares, even if for just a little while.

So, turn the page, my friend. Enter the Land of Stories and lose yourself in another world; a world where you don't have to search to find great stories, because they're everywhere you look.

Forget what the know-it-alls try to tell you. Great stories are not extinct. THEY DO EXIST!

FIRST PLACE

NONA
©2006 by Claire Grasse

She smelled smoke. She set the bottle of lemon oil on the coffee table and went to the kitchen, still clutching the rag she had been using to polish the furniture. The kitchen was burning: thick curtains of smoke boiling along the walls, orange flames like live creatures leaping and hissing at the ceiling. For some reason, as an offering maybe, she threw the rag into the flames the way you'd throw a bone to a vicious dog so you could get away...

She turned to run, but her hip gave way, and she stumbled. Someone laughed, and behind her the flames howled and nipped at her back.

"Over here, Mamaw!"

She turned her head and saw her great-grandson in the dining room, his black hair slicked back and furrowed with comb tracks, wearing dirty jeans, a white T-shirt with the sleeves ripped out, and pushing a lawn mower, of all things. He pushed it toward her, grinning like a wolf.

"Hop on! I see you left another pot burning on the stove!" he said merrily, and laughed again. "I'm afraid you'll have to go with me. Come on, hop on and I'll push you to the nursing home. Your room's all ready; it's even got cable TV!"

His laughter blended with the shriek of the fire, and then they were the same sound....

The woman woke with a start, the blood rushing in her ears, the sheet twisted around her legs, and the sun shining in the window like a prayer.

She pulled herself to a sitting position and swung her legs over the side of the bed. The wind-up alarm clock on the night stand pointed toward six forty-five. She had tried before to learn the luxury of sleeping late, but couldn't get the knack of it. She had risen early all her life, to do otherwise felt vaguely sinful. She'd sleep when she was dead. Plenty of time then.

Her clothes were hanging from a peg on the back of the bathroom door. The morning routine was short and without unnecessary fuss. She made a cup of tea and a piece of toast and took them to the kitchen table, where she ate watching the cardinals at the feeder outside her window and listening to the peaceful ticking of the wall clock.

When her cup and plate were rinsed, she went back to tidy her room.

For twenty years, the rituals had been the same. This morning, however, she stopped for a minute when the bed was made, and picked up the ivory hand-mirror that lay on the vanity next to the matching boar's-hair brush. Scraps of the dream fluttered at the edges of her thoughts like stubborn threads unraveling from a hem. She peered uneasily at her reflection, as if she might see the future in the spotted surface.

Black eyes looked back at her from a face that was as furrowed and brown as the shell of a walnut. Twin silver braids hung over her shoulders to lie on flattened breasts. She looked like a squaw from an ancient Indian legend. Her Pa was a white sharecropper, but she favored Ma, a half-breed Blackfoot.

Nowadays, though, no one was allowed to say "half-breed," or even "Injun." Now that ancestrys like hers had come into fashion, people said "Native American" and children from the elementary school came around to interview her for their reports and projects.

She didn't understand all the fuss herself. She recollected when it had been a shame—near unto a crime—to be neither one race nor the other. Well. There was no denying that times had changed.

There was nothing in the mirror but the reminder of a long past. She put it carefully away.

She left the house, and stood a minute under the live oak by the front porch. The dust of the yard puffed gently around her canvas shoes and settled over them in a fine, white shower. The woman shielded her eyes and surveyed the sky. The temperature was nearing ninety and last night's dew was still on the grass. The sky was clear, though: an aggressive blue, with none of the ominous haze that bespoke a day thick with humidity. The birds were flying high, too, and the promise of a breeze whispered through the wisteria that dripped like purple honey from the eaves.

She dropped her hand and shuffled off to visit the goats, her faded, cotton work shirt already dampening between her shoulder blades.

The goats were all nannies. Billies were ornery, sometimes downright mean, and anyway, she was past birthing livestock in the middle of the night. Three was all she needed to keep the brush in check, and maybe give the sense at sunset that there was something friendly nearby when the dark was closing in.

The goats came running when she called, and she stroked their heads while she checked the water in the long trough and fed them a little salt for a treat. She ran her hands over their short, rough hair and they butted their knobby heads against her legs. She visited with them a bit, breathing in their sharp outdoor-scent, while the white one nibbled at her shirttail.

At last, reluctantly, she pushed them away and walked to the tool shed.

The shed smelled of dry rot and two-cycle engine oil. Cobwebs draped the beams and swung in the draft of the open door. Mud-dauber nests sprouted from the door frame, and the unmistakable scrabbling of mice came from the unfinished loft overhead. She stood still, trying to remember what was stored up there, because she'd sure never make it up there now to find out.

Tack, she decided, from farm horses long dead. Or, old sacks of feed gone moldy with age. She had a sudden, clear recollection of sifting through bags of horse feed with Tanny Colson, her childhood friend, looking for pieces of molasses-coated corn to crack between their teeth. Her eyes crinkled with the memory.

A shiny, red lawnmower crouched in the back corner, and she eyed it with distaste. Dewey had bought it for her. Goats, he'd insisted, weren't enough to keep the property in order. She hated the machine with its manic roar that seemed to shake the birds from the trees, and its foul perfume of gas and exhaust that lingered in the air and settled on the flowers. It seeped into her pores if she stood too close, so that her skin smelled acrid and dirty for hours afterward.

Dewey would be over to mow as soon as the grass was dry, and that would be the end of peace, at least for the morning. She glared at the machine and reached for a hoe.

The garden covered a quarter-acre behind the house. She saw that deer had been at the lettuce again. Well now, there was no harm in that. The winter crops had long bolted in the heat anyway. She stooped and, balancing herself on the hoe, pulled up the six remaining lettuces by the roots and tossed them over the fence where her midnight visitors could find them without trampling down the pole beans and okra. She moved a few rows over, pulling up the last of the broccoli and cabbages, sending them over the fence for the deer, too.

Harold would have said she was crazy as a coon for feeding those pests. Then he'd have sat up all night with a shotgun full of rock salt, watching the garden just to spite her. She considered Harold for a moment, then bent over again and wrenched up a handful of tender carrots. She sent them over the fence after the others and hoped that Harold, God rest him, saw her do it. Satisfied, she turned to hoeing the corn.

She was staking the tomatoes when she heard Dewey's truck crunch up the drive. He slammed the truck door, and a moment later she heard him knocking at her front door. She let him knock as she tied up a few spindly branches and gathered some young onions. Finally, when she couldn't think of anything else to do, she collected her hoe and met him stomping around the back corner to look for her.

"Mornin', Mamaw!" He dropped a noisy kiss on her cheek and took the hoe.

"Mornin' yourself. You come alone?"

"Yep. One of the nurses' aides called in sick, so June had to cover the shift."

Thank the Lord for small favors, she thought. That tart he lived with hadn't got two sensible thoughts in her head. A day spent in her company was as good as wasted.

She opened the front door and the cool of the house, dim and smelling of sixty years' worth of chicken dinners, underlaid with liniment, and a suggestion of Irish Spring soap, swallowed them.

She dropped the onions on the drainboard. "Can you stay to dinner?"

"Long as I'm back at the shop by one. I got a customer coming in with a bad tranny, needs to be changed out. It's gonna take me and the new guy all the rest of today to do."

"Well, you'll be wore out if you mow first. You can come back another time. That grass'll keep."

"Nah, I'm all right. Won't take me but a hour 'n a half, two hours."

She wasn't one to mollycoddle. "Take you some water then."

"I got a jug in the truck." He left, whistling good-naturedly through his teeth and letting the door slam shut behind him.

The mustang grapes were thick on the south fence this summer, and the woman had picked a bushel basketfull the day before, pulling the basket behind her on an old Radio Flyer wagon as she moved down the vines. She dragged it in now from the laundry room and tried to hoist it into the sink. She got it to waist height, but she couldn't lift it higher. It dropped on her foot, spilling a good quart of grapes onto the floor, where they rolled in all directions.

She set the basket flat, and studied it a minute, thinking. Danged if she'd call Dewey to lift it for her. He'd have her drying up in June's old folk's home before sundown.

Outside, the mower roared to life, crowding into her head and her ears. Her china teacups trembled on the hutch in the dining room. For a moment, the world was filled with the throb and snarl of the motor, and then he must have moved around back because the noise faded to a distant thrumming.

She pulled a kitchen chair over to the sink and got the basket up onto the seat. She considered again, and then dragged over another chair. Balancing herself carefully on the drainboard, she stood on the second chair. She bent, lifted the basket from the chair to the sink, and tipped it in with a little *"huh"* of victory. She set the basket carefully on the counter, and climbed down, shaky, mindful of her balance.

She put away the chairs and swept the spilled grapes into the dustbin, then rinsed and picked over the fruit. When she was done, her hands and apron were stained purple and the big kettle was full. She added a little water and tried to heft it. It was too heavy.

Well, nuts to that. She wasn't helpless by a long stretch, though *some* folks liked to think so. Reluctantly, she left it by the sink. Dewey'd have to shift it for her; there was no way around it.

She peeled potatoes and laid strips of salt pork in flour. By the time he came in, smelling of sweat and exhaust, she was setting out silverware and plates of hot food.

"Gaw, it's hotter'n Hell's backside out there!" He wiped his face on his T-shirt and drew a glass of water, which he drained in one noisy breath.

Her nose twitched a little. "Goin' to rain this evenin.'"

He drew another glass, drank half, then set it down, shaking his head. "Nah, it ain't. Paper said ten percent chance today, and they's no clouds out there." He ducked his face under the faucet and scrubbed vigorously.

Her nose twitched again. It *was* going to rain. She could smell it on him, but she said nothing further. Later, when June complained of the downpour on her newly-waxed car, he'd say— believing it himself—that he had told Mamaw at lunch how it looked like rain.

She handed him a towel. "You can fetch that kettle of grapes to the stove for me. I got room for it now." She looked at him sideways, but he seemed to think nothing of the favor and lifted it over obediently.

"You makin' jelly?"

"Ayuh." She turned the flame on low and sat down at the table.

Dewey forked slices of fried salt pork onto his plate. "June wants you to come for supper Sunday."

"All right."

He looked at her sideways. "I can pick you up 'bout five."

"I'll drive myself."

He let it go, and she was glad.

He ate quickly, with little conversation, and finished a slice of lemon pie before he stood to leave. She went to the pantry, pulled twenty dollars out of the old tin lard bucket, and held it out to him.

He shook his head. "I ain't taking your money, Mamaw. I don't mind to cut grass." He slapped his stomach and laughed. "Keeps me from goin' to seed."

These were steps to a familiar dance. She fussed a little, then put the money away. He left in a boisterous clamor of banging doors and spraying gravel.

After he'd gone, she moved around the silent kitchen, washing the dishes and wiping the table. She set away the leftovers and pulled a mason jar of sweet tea from the back of the icebox. She wrapped it carefully in a towel and put it in a plastic grocery sack, along with a dozen molasses cookies in waxed paper. She checked the grapes. They were swelling and giving off their juices, and a faint steam hovered on the surface of the pot. She gave them a stir, turned off the flame, and went out; noticing with some annoyance that Dewey'd left the lawnmower parked by the rose bushes again.

It appeared to be grinning at her, wolflike, and she gave it a wide berth.

The sun sat on her neck like something alive and beat on the earth, pulling the hot smells of ripe grass and cedar into the air, driving the cicadas to a frenzied, electric buzzing. Most folks hereabouts hide from the heat; hate it like a sworn enemy. They speak of summer as something to hunker down against and endure. Summer in Texas means drought, wildfires, shriveled crops, and gaping cracks in the ground where the earth pulls in on itself from the long, brutal force of the sun.

She knew all this, had felt it herself, but still she welcomed the summers. She could stand outside, stretch, and feel the heat baking the sickness and weakness from her bones, leaving her clean from the inside out, driving the chill from her body and soul. She liked that she alone, of everyone she knew, felt this way. It was as if the sun, in all its brutality and blessing, belonged to her.

She crossed the back of her property and struck onto a path worn smooth in the meadow. The grass was high and painted over with Mexican hats, Indian blankets, and a tall, pretty flower people used to call butter-and-eggs. Wild thyme grew thick underfoot, the scent of it rising where she stepped, sharp and haunting, like a memory out of reach.

The path left the meadow at the edge of Sawyer's property. A deep creek ran out of the woods a quarter-mile away. Back when she was a girl, Mason Sawyer had dammed it up at this corner to make a good-sized fishing pond.

She found the long stone bench still sitting, after all these years, under the redbud tree. She lowered herself gingerly onto the seat, remembering when Mr. Sawyer had it moved here all the way from California by train. Had it been eighty years ago?

That was the year they built the new schoolhouse, with indoor bathrooms and electricity. Vance Claymore stood against it, she recollected. Said electricity was the devil's work and no decent person would do their bathroom business inside of a house, or a school for that matter. He sent his girls, though, when it was built, same's the rest of the town.

She chuckled a little, remembering. Lord. So many people dead and gone.

She unwrapped her jar of tea and took a long drink, pressing the cold towel to her neck and face. A movement caught the corner of her eye, and she turned to look. Three feet away, a slim, green garter snake poured itself through the grass and disappeared into the meadow. The sight of it raised another memory so sweet and sudden she caught her breath with the force of it.

She was thirteen years old, and Teddy Jinks, who everybody called Hijinks, brought a bull snake to school and chased her screaming around the schoolyard until her braids came untied and her hair flew loose, while all the boys rolled on the ground, laughing fit to bust.

The teacher made him stay after school a whole week cleaning blackboards for it. She loved Teddy Jinks ever since. When she was fourteen, he took her horseback riding during the summer break. At fifteen, he brought her sticks of peppermint candy from Jape's Mercantile, and they fished in the stream down behind the Methodist church. And when she turned sixteen, he kissed her right here at the edge of Sawyer's pond.

She closed her eyes and pressed the tea jar to her throat, pulling the memory from her mind strand by strand. How had they come to be here? She disremembered that part, but could see him now, reaching up with one hand to grab a low branch, while tilting her chin with the other, before leaning in to kiss her.

The ducks on the pond startled at their presence then. Maybe they had felt it with her, how the earth seemed to shift a little underfoot and the sky to tilt. For one long moment there was nothing in the world but the taste of his mouth, the splash of water, and the swift, sudden flight of mergansers taking wing.

She packed up the jar of tea and painfully stood to go.

Teddy was killed right after that in one of those terrible farm accidents that folks talked of in hushed voices after the children were in bed. She had grieved alone in her room, keening into her pillow like a wild thing when no one was around to hear.

When Harold Straybeck, who owned the hardware store and had soft, white hands like a city woman, started calling twice a week with his bunches of hothouse pansies and his talk of maybe buying her mama an icebox for the kitchen, she finally accepted him, thinking at sixteen that persistence might be a worthy substitute for love.

She struck out again, cross-lots through Sawyer's back field, a little slower now, feeling the force of the afternoon sun. Across the field, Jesse's house shimmered in the waves of heat rising from the parched grasses. He saw her from his chair on the screened back porch and waved. She lifted her hand in reply.

Jesse Greenwood had been her friend time out of mind. Their mothers had helped each other hoe sweet potatoes and put up watermelon preserves back when Mrs. Greenwood was the only white woman who wanted what to do with the timid half-breed wife of a mean drunk. She and Jesse had each married and buried a lot of kinfolk together over the years, and she favored him now more than most of her own kin.

She toiled up the back steps and opened the screen door.

Jesse was in his wicker rocker, whittling at a bar of Ivory soap. "You crazy old woman," he greeted her. "What the devil are you doin' out in this heat?"

She dropped her bag and sat heavily in the matching chair, fanning herself. Moses, the old black spaniel, crept out from under the coffee table and greeted her, thumping his tail on the floor when she scratched behind his ears.

"I'm out checkin' to make sure you ain't up and died in the night. Watch who you're callin' old."

He chuckled and set aside the soap, reaching for his walker.

She waved him back into his seat. "Set still. I'll get my own drink in a minute. Just need to catch my breath."

He picked up his whittling again. "You should have drove over. It's hot enough to kill Satan out there."

"I guess I'm still tougher'n him, then."

She pulled herself to her feet and took the bag into the kitchen. She found glasses in the cupboard and washed them good, because Jesse never did get his dishes more than half-clean. She filled them from the jug of tea in the icebox and arranged her molasses cookies on a plate. She put it all on a tray and carried it to the back porch.

"You seen that new shop opened up by Hanpeter's Fabrics?" He asked her.

She fed Moses a cookie. "No, what is it?"

"Some kinda witchy hocus-pocus voodoo place. Sells crystal balls and incense and Weejee boards. Cripes, Carol got her cards read, or some nonsense like that the other day."

She felt her ears prick with interest. "You mean like fortune-telling?"

He pointed the knife at her. "That's it. Like them old ladies that used to set up booths at the county fair and they'd tell your future for a nickel."

"You believe in things like that?"

He looked offended. "Hell, no. And the Lord don't like it, neither. The Bible says so."

She waved that off and sipped at her tea. There wasn't much the Lord *did* like, as far as she could tell. She suddenly wished she'd brought her car, and her pocketbook.

"I heard Mavis Simms fell and broke her hip," Jesse was saying.

She pushed the new shop to the back of her mind and gave him her attention. "When'd that happen?"

"Monday mornin'. They didn't find her until her daughter stopped to pick her up for prayer meeting Wednesday night."

He spoke with grim relish, and a little shiver walked up her spine. A broken hip was the bogeyman. If that happened, you were through, it was the nursing home for you, and everyone knew it. You'd spend what months were left to you in a wheelchair parked in some yellow hallway that stank of urine and canned green beans, surrounded by silent husks of people in diapers.

She changed the subject quickly, and they talked of other things for the better part of an hour. The cookies were almost gone when they heard the front door open and a woman holler "Yoo-hoo!" down the hallway.

Jesse paled. "Oh Lord, put them cookies away! It's Carol and she's come to check my sugar."

She understood at once and slid the plate with the last two cookies under the low table. Moses thumped his tail appreciatively.

A tall, broad-shouldered redhead in nursing scrubs filled the doorway. "Well, Nona Straybeck! I didn't see your car out front. Did June drop you off?"

The old woman glared sideways at Jesse. If he said a word about her walking here, she'd tell about the cookies. Jesse buried his face in his tea, silent.

"Oh, you could say that," she answered vaguely. "How's Max doing?"

Carol shook her head. Her husband of thirty years had bone cancer, and everyone knew it was just a matter of time. "He's fair," she answered. "Good days and bad days. You know how it is."

She did, for a fact.

Carol looked at her watch and unzipped an insulated bag of supplies. "You ready, Grandpa?"

Jesse grunted and held out his arm, looking out the window over the fields toward Sawyer's pond.

Nona excused herself to the bathroom, where she dallied as long as she could. It always made her uneasy to see Jesse Greenwood, who'd once built bridges and roads, and broke horses better than any man in the county, sit passive under needles and test strips and cotton gauze; the trappings of medicine reducing a big, full life to one of infirmity and need.

When she came back, Carol was packing up her bag.

"Nona, can I give you a lift home? Or is June coming back by for you?"

"I might take a ride, thank you." She gathered her bag with its jar half-full of warm tea and winked at Jesse. "Watch your sugar now, Jesse."

He gave her a look. "Stay out of the sun, Nona."

She laughed aloud, and followed Carol to her car.

The house was very still when she got back. Even the humming of the air conditioner and the ticking of the clock seemed a part of the silence. She sank down onto the worn easy chair and passed a hand over her face. Mercy, that walk had taken it out of her, more than she'd want to admit to anyone. She really was too old to be traipsing around like a gypsy. She thought of starting on the jelly before it got too late. She didn't want to be all evening with it.

Then she remembered the fortune-teller Jesse'd told her about. She wondered what it cost to have a future told, and how much future there was to see for a tough and tired old woman with better than ninety years behind her. She laid her head back on the recliner and breathed out, watching the light and shade play across the wall. In a minute, when she was rested, she might get her pocketbook and go find out. Maybe there were things in a crystal ball that would frighten her. But then, she thought dimly, she'd seen a lot of good and terrible things in her lifetime, and she wasn't likely to run from shadows now...

When she woke, there were thunderheads building on the horizon, and the sun through the window was the worn gold of a late summer evening. The shadows on the wall were stretching themselves together to fill the corners and edges of the room.

Someone was here with her, she could sense it. She turned her head a little. "Dewey? June?"

The young man that walked around and stood before her chair was broad-shouldered and handsome and his eyes shone with fun. He tipped his cloth cap back on his head with a gesture so familiar it sent a sob to her throat.

"Well, hello, Nona Bennett. Remember me?"

She stared for a long moment, and then stretched out her hand, shaking. "Teddy?"

"It's been a long time, I've missed you."

"Oh, Teddy!" her voice trembled and broke, and she covered

her mouth.

He grinned at her. "I'm on my way to see if the fish are biting down at Sawyer's pond. I thought I'd see if you were ready to join me." He held out his hand, and she took it unquestioningly.

He pulled her to her feet, and she came to him, laughing and sobbing, with no aches or twinges or the stiff creaking of stubborn joints. They stood a moment, their fingers just touching, and she noticed that her own hands and arms were smooth and full, fairly throbbing with life and joy. She touched her throat. The wrinkles, the folds of loose skin, where had they gone?

Teddy pressed the backs of his fingers to her cheek. "Are you ready, Nona?"

She was still gasping, half-laughing with the mystery of it. "Am I dead?"

He threw his head back and gave the shout of laughter that she had heard so often, and remembered all the long years between them. "Dead? Oh, honey. Come with me, and see."

She tangled her fingers in his, and strength pulsed through her like music. They stepped through the wall and into the old light of the fading day, past the red lawnmower parked harmlessly by the rose bush. She looked down at it as they passed. Had it ever frightened her?

Behind them, the sun shone thin and gold on the bottoms of the storm clouds, and in the living room, the shadows gathered strength, and fell.

About the author:

Claire Grasse is thirty-something and lives in Central Texas with her husband of fifteen years, her four children, two dogs and a cat. Besides writing, her hobbies include soap making, hiking, and playing the Irish Pennywhistle. Her short story Nona reflects her fascination with the old-fashioned rhythms of life and speech in generations past.

SECOND PLACE

WHAT WE ARE MADE OF
©2006 by Mia Lazarewicz

Today, tonight, toafternoon—what the hell is 4:15 pm, anyway?

"Late afternoon" is a bullshit phrase, and so is "the good fight." Well, it *was* a good fight. You put up a good fight, Sarah, in the late afternoon of today and tonight. I think I should have known by now that you'd never give a shred less than your whole, but we are always learning, even at the end of our years.

What I learned, after I stopped being angry, is that this time was no different. What I learned is that I should not have underestimated you. You were giving your whole, your everything. But the everything in you finally ran dry, and it took us fifty-seven years to get there. I witnessed you, and you witnessed me, for fifty-seven years.

I'm writing this to tell you everything I never told you in the past. These are my secrets, the ones I kept even from you, because they ran deeper in me than anyone could ever understand. They are what reside within my eyes, my ears, my fingertips. They are the actual reasons I find you impossible to let go of. They are your truth.

When the gallon of milk runs out, you can shake the bottle over your cereal, but the fact remains that half of your corn flakes will sit on top, unfulfilled, desperately yearning to snatch a few drops, while those at the bottom become inedibly soppy. I also discovered that, after fifty-seven years together, what it all boils down to is that you are the empty gallon of milk and I am the depleted bowl of corn flakes.

Probably when we were honeymooners, I would have said you were the sun, moon, and stars in my incomplete Milky Way. I would have compared you to roses, to the sound of church bells, to the smell of freshly mown grass (my favorite things—yes, I remember when you led me outside and we had sex on the newly-cut lawn).

I guess that's what carried us fifty-seven years. And now you are the expired dairy expulsions from a bovine, and I am a shredded, lonely, uncomfortably soggy heap of corn flakes.

Through my grief, however, I've found I can recall only a happy haze. Even our most acerbic fights remind me of the fire that spurred you. Your flaws were like raisins in an oatmeal cookie. Yes, I would have preferred chocolate chips, but when you've got cookies, what do the details matter? You are still a cookie—warm, sugary, unhealthy in the best way possible; always bringing a smile and satisfaction.

Forgive me for saying *flaws*—you know I have always been jealous of everything you were. You were self-absorbed, but I would have killed for your self-confidence. You were loud, but I wish people heard me the way they listened to you. You were vain, but I couldn't stop looking at you, either.

I loved Scrabble. My friends and I used to have weekly Scrabble tournaments; losers paid for the pizza and beer. Usually it was just three or four of us, testosterone raging through a mental battle of wits. But I guess you loved me for it. My God, I'll never forget the night Jake invited you to play. We were stunned to see a strange woman at the table when we arrived. I'd hardly removed my coat before you tossed me a beer. You *tossed* me a beer! You'd inhaled a slice of pizza before I'd even gotten to the table.

Well, I knew you'd be toast.

VORTEX. Jesus Christ, you just played VORTEX. For forty-nine points! I'd just gotten thirty-two points for FLAXEN and thought I'd won the game. And then you go and play VORTEX on my FLAXEN for a triple word score. I remember that infuriating little smile that played across your lips, as you silently dared me to call you on it. I used to see that same smile when we played pool together. You were an awful pool player, but when you hit an accidental shot you'd twitch the corners of your lips and swagger around the table as though you knew bouncing the two-ball off three rails would tip it just into the corner pocket. Luck did not play a part in your life; your skills were simply that formidable. You were only missing those easy shots to make the game closer. I appreciated your efforts.

You were the first woman who ever beat me in Scrabble. Not to sound chauvinistic, but I had never met you before, and you were a woman, and you had just beaten me in Scrabble. I remember staring at you across the table, resenting everything about you. I hated the way your hair fell softly around your cheekbones, I hated your graceful collarbone, and I hated your elegant fingers when they smoothed your shirt down over your sensational breasts. I hated the spark in your eyes, the rasp in your voice, the viciousness of your speech. I hated watching your fiery lips as they tortured me into submission. I had to leave the room.

"Leaving already? I'll play you again, if you wish."

I hated how your eyes beckoned and teased me, hated how your voice slowly coated me from top to bottom.

"I just need a drink."

I stopped hating you after you fixed me the dirtiest martini my body could handle.

I have never told you that had you not beat me in Scrabble that day, I would not even have noticed you were at the table. Your scintillating smarts struck me as a bull charges a matador. I waved the FLAXEN *capote,* and you attacked with your VORTEX *cuernos.* You gored me.

Now that you are gone, I will reluctantly admit in this letter that you were better than me at Scrabble. Somewhere, you are smiling, and the mere thought of your smile is why I have lived as happily as I have. When I could see it in person, I felt like dropping to my knees. Your easy grin inspired me. Look at this. You have reduced me to a cliché. How many times did this happen?

"Look," you sighed. *"He's just a friend. He's an old friend, we talk occasionally, we grab drinks once in a while, he tells me I'm still the prettiest girl he knows. Why wouldn't I stay friends with him? Oh, well, I guess the sex is pretty good, too. "*

"For once, can you not make a joke? I'm jealous, you know I'm jealous, and your way of appeasing me is to joke that the sex is pretty good?"

"John, you're being ridiculous. "

That was your way of trivializing my problems. You would tell me I was being ridiculous, that my feelings were petty and unjustified. You knew it nearly killed me to hear how he told you you're beautiful. My God, were you beautiful. I told you all the time, but I understand it means more from others. I understand you wanted to keep me jealous. I hated your games. I hated them because they worked, because you knew they worked, because you knew I'd try harder to make sure you were appreciated.

"I am not being ridiculous. I hate it when you play games with me. Who cares if he thinks you're pretty? I'm the one you're living with, the one who gets to touch you, to fantasize about you. Every goddamn day, you nearly kill me with your sexiness. You know that? You nearly kill me."

"Awww, thank you," you purred. *"You're the sweetest guy I've ever met. I love you even more when you're grumpy and jealous."*

Game, set, and match.

I don't have a favorite memory of you because you *are* my favorite memory. I never kept a picture of you at work. Did you know that? I didn't tell you this, but I bought a bottle of your body wash to keep at my office.

I would sneak it into the bathroom and wash my hands with it when I needed to have you around me. Your scent would linger, women would tell me I smelled good, and those wavy scents blurred the clock. It was never too long before I could go home, because it just always seemed you were standing behind me, draping your arms across my chest, pressing your breasts into my shoulder blades. I hated how you knew you could get anything you wanted when you stood behind me like that.

Do you know when I started believing in destiny? When I was watching you move down the aisle, leaning heavily on your father's arm for support. Not because of the whole you-were-so-beautiful-I-couldn't-feel-my-toes thing. Not because of the I-knew-this-was-the-beginning-of-the-rest-of-my-life thing. Not because of the I-can't-believe-I-found-someone-who-actually-wants-to-marry-me thing. It was because when you made it up to the altar, and took your place next to me, you whispered, "*John. It turns out that four shots of tequila is too many before you have to walk down your wedding aisle.*"

It was destiny, because I had been drinking tequila, too.

Neither of us particularly remembers our wedding day. Everyone else was appalled, while we were still laughing about it just a week ago. Only a week ago? It seems I haven't seen you in ages. You understood that as long as you and I were on the same page, who cares if it was a publicly-intoxicated page? Impressing other people was never on your list of priorities.

"*Do you remember my nana's face when I fell over on the dance floor?*"

"*That was amazing. Have you looked at our wedding pictures recently?*"

"*Yes, all the time. My favorite one is where you're holding me and my dress up. Strapless dress plus too many drinks equals many members of our wedding party saw my tits.*"

"*Yes, but they are such great tits.*"

"*Yes, they are.*"

I miss your tits, Sarah.

We were both too selfish to have kids. Our poor parents were hoping for tons of grandkids, but instead they got tons of postcards from every continent on Earth. We used our money to travel, and though everyone said we would, we never regretted our choice not to have kids. Instead, we have full picture albums for every country we've ever been to. In Egypt, we scrawled our names in the sand, and in Greece we played Statues until the sun went down. We tried to walk the Great Wall and made out underwater next to the Great Barrier Reef. In France, we chain-smoked and you stopped shaving your armpits to get a "feel for the country."

One night, in Paris, we went dancing at a tiny cafe *au Champs-Elysee*. There was no music, but you pulled me off my chair to a clear space by the sidewalk. You made me twirl you and, clear as day, I can see your Parisian skirt floating around your legs. One by one, the other customers put down their forks and turned in their chairs to watch. With anyone else, in any other time, and any other place, I would have been mortified. With you, I was on the proverbial cloud nine. You never failed to remind me how inexplicably lucky I was to have you. I was dancing on the streets of Paris with my wife, your perfect legs, a shining moon, and a captivated audience.

Then I realized that no one was watching me—they were all watching you.

Jealous, and suddenly self-conscious, I gave you a finishing dip and we strolled back to our table amid smiles and scattered applause. One man followed us there.

'*Vous êtes la dame la plus belle que j'ai jamais vue.* "

"*What the hell did he just say? Sarah, want me to punch him?*"

"*Shut up, Andy. Ah, merci, bel étranger. S'il vous plaît, un baiser.*"

"*Qui est-il?*"

"*Ne vous inquiétez pas. Il est seulement un ami de moi.*"

"*What did you just say? Since when do you speak French?*"

And then you kissed him. Look, thirty years later, I learned how to say this: *Tu l'as embrassé bien devant moi.* You kissed him right in front of me, *depuis longtemps. Salope.*

You told him I was your friend. I didn't know that's what you told him. I didn't know what that entire conversation meant for ten years, until I got up the courage to ask.

The worst part about the whole thing? Just when I was starting to think you could not be any more attractive, I heard you speaking French. I should have hated you for kissing him, and I did, but I loved you so much more because you were always surprising me.

A friend. We'd been married for twenty years at that point, and you told him I was your friend! Only you could make me feel the way I did that day.

When I was a boy I had a dog. He went from perfectly healthy companion to canine corpse in three weeks to the day. He had a cancer that decimated his body, and we were the innocent group of bystanders, witnesses to the crash.

When people would try to console me that a quick death is so much easier to handle than a slow, drawn-out death, I would agree with them.

"Yes, poor Dexter didn't have to suffer very long. I'm grateful for that."

The thought of my dog suffering was worse to me than the thought of him dying. But when you were in the hospital for so long, living out your days, your months, all I wanted was for you to be suffering. If you were suffering, it meant you were still alive and still had feelings. And if you were still alive and still had feelings, it meant you were still around to love me. Selfish as it may have been, I needed nothing more in the world than for you to love me. I do not know if that is why you fought "the good fight." I would like to think it is.

I hated you the most in my whole life when you left me. When you died, I thought I could never forgive you. I wanted to pound your body, beat you senseless, and make you cry. I could spend the rest of my life writing about you, and yet I suddenly feel as though

I have nothing more to say right now. But we had a lifetime together; we stood up and took notice together. We defied the odds. And so, not now, but in the future, I will write you more letters. When I need to cry, or laugh, or simply remember, I will write you more letters. I will write to you every time the loneliness begins to pick at me. I will continue to be your witness. And, now that you are doing other things, I will continue to be mine.

About the author:

Mia Lazarewicz is a 21-year-old senior at Tulane University, lifelong gymnast, and avid Red Sox fan. She's a brilliant decision maker, as long as she never has to choose between a stiff drink and a hearty meal. Mia idolizes John Steinbeck and judges people who've never read a Harry Potter novel. She's good at heating microwave dinners, sarcasm, and ruining pictures. Mia can beat below average Scrabble players and will never shy from a good debate. She strongly believes that everyone should speak several languages; and is obsessed with good grammar, though she refuses to use the word *whom* because she doesn't know how. She's never had any writing published, unless you count the tests her mother hung on the refrigerator. She hopes to inspire people to think for themselves, fight worthwhile battles, and read all they can find.

THIRD PLACE

A LAKE IN THE PARK
©2006 by John M. Bourne

Like many Grandfathers, George loved telling stories to his grandchildren. When they wanted a story, they would climb on his lap and demand, "Story! Story!" Granddad would soon give in and always asked what they wanted a story about; they could choose any subject they liked. Some of the stories were true, most were fiction made up spontaneously. He told stories about the sun and the stars, a seagull, a garage, a table leg and a worm, among other things.

One day his five-year-old granddaughter Rebecca jumped on Granddad's lap and demanded a story. After a little persuasion, he gave in and invited her to choose a subject. She asked for a story about the lake in Queens Park in Brighton, on the south coast of England. They had visited the park on the day before and walked round the lake.

This is the story he told:

When I was a little boy, I went to school at Queens Park School just down the road from the park. The area looked rather different then. The school looks very much the same now, but the area around it was very different. In fact, it was in a bit of a state. The war hadn't long been over and some bombs had fallen in the area, destroying several houses. The local people wanted something done about the bombsites, but the council couldn't afford it for the time being, so they had to put up with a lot of rubble and mess in between some of the houses. The houses either side of the bomb sites had great big wooden supports holding their walls up where once another house had stood. Fences had been put round the sites and notices saying,

KEEP OUT
Dangerous and Unstable Surfaces

At the school, we were all forbidden to go on the sites. If we did and got caught, we were in serious trouble. In those days, trouble meant being made to bend over and then hit with a cane, anything from one to six times. The canes the teachers used were thin, bendy bamboo cane that really stung!

My best friend was Jim. Jim and I were both twelve and full of mischief. We had just started smoking. We thought it was clever then—we know now how dangerous it is, but no one knew then. If we got caught at school or at home we would be in big trouble. We couldn't afford many cigarettes, just a few Players Weights, as they were called, and we used to smoke them round the back of the bike shed in the playground, where we hoped no one could see.

One day, on our way to school we met an old man struggling with his shopping. Being kind and helpful boys (well, sometimes) we offered to help the old man and carried his shopping home for him. We got chatting and he told us how he had lived in the area all his life. He'd seen soldiers going off to the First World War and returning: some injured, some stricken by gas; and of course, they were many who didn't return at all.

He described to us some of the dogfights he had seen in the sky over Brighton in the Second World War as Spitfires and Hurricanes tried to shoot down the German heavy bombers. He was at home alone on the day the Germans bombed his part of the town, and some of the bombs fell all round him. He ran out of his house and hid in an upturned bath in his back garden. It was just was well that he did because his house was damaged and all the people next door were killed. He then talked of the fires that the bombs started and described the difficult and dangerous search through the rubble for survivors.

Like you, we loved a good story and were fascinated at his so much that we forgot the time, and were late for school and both of us got the cane for that!

When the old man was telling us about the bombs, he had pointed out his house and was able to tell us who had lived in the houses that were destroyed. One of the buildings had been a tobacco shop, and he pointed out where it stood.

When Jim and I met later at playtime, we discussed the possibility of trying to get into what was left of the shop in case there were any cigarettes left. We decided to have a look after school. We were really excited about it and couldn't concentrate all day long as we waited for the time to pass.

When school was over, we left as usual, slipped away from the other children, and hung around until the coast was clear. Then we climbed quickly over the fence and into the bombsite. Parts of walls were still standing and we had a good look around, getting filthy in the process. We found nothing. We looked for a staircase in the hope there might be stairs leading down into a cellar. Eventually, we found the bottom of the stairs but there were none going down. We were on the point of giving up when I put my foot down and it went through the floor near the back of the site, against what remained of the rear wall. After pulling bricks and rubble out of the way until there was a gap big enough to get through, we couldn't see what was down there. There was only one way to find out: we lowered ourselves through the gap and, summoning our courage, dropped down into the darkness.

It seemed a long time before we hit the floor hard, jarring every bone in our bodies. It was absolutely pitch black down there, but being smokers, we had some matches. We looked round and found some old files and some boxes of sweets, all ruined by water, but no cigarettes.

Then we saw a big wooden cupboard stretching right up to the ceiling. It was locked, but we found some pieces of old pipe and broke the lock. Inside the cupboard were cigarettes, thousands of cigarettes, packed up from floor to ceiling. We did a dance of delight, whooping like Indians preparing for battle in the old westerns. When we calmed down, we saw that the cigarettes were mostly Players Weights, but there were some John Players as well. Water had got into the cupboard, but because the packets were all wrapped in cellophane most of them were fine.

We stuffed our pockets with as many as we could carry and then tried to get out. We couldn't reach the gap we had got through and there was nothing to stand on. In the end, we had to get the bits of pipe and make holes in the wall to climb up. Fortunately, it wasn't too hard because the plaster was rotten and the wall was already damaged. We had just enough matches to light our way out.

As we climbed, we could see through holes in the wall into another part of the cellar complex. It was very dark, almost impossible to make anything out, but we thought we could see something metallic and big; we just couldn't see it well enough.

It might have been part of an office chair, or a gas cylinder, but it could have been an unexploded bomb! Being children, we thought it *had* to be a bomb and were very excited about it. We wanted to tell everyone about it, but keep the cigarettes to ourselves. We decided to suppress our excitement. The bomb, if that's what it was, wasn't going anywhere. No one was allowed on the site and we had the opportunity to make some money with the cigarettes.

The next day in break-time, Jim and I flashed some of our cigarettes around and it wasn't long before some of the others asked us about them. We told them we had a good supply and were willing to sell them at a very reasonable price. Back then, cigarettes in the shops cost about one shilling for ten (five pence in today's money, or about ten US cents). We had an assortment of packets in tens and twenties, which we were prepared to sell for nine pence for ten, and one shilling and six pence for twenty (eight cents for ten, fifteen cents for twenty).

We soon did a roaring trade and ran out very quickly. We took orders, then, promising delivery the next day. We went back into school very pleased with ourselves. The only trouble was that some of the teachers noticed all the cigarettes around and were not pleased. Our Form Teacher came in and said if he found out who was selling cheap cigarettes, they would be in serious trouble! We know what that meant and my backside tingled at the very thought of it!

We were too brave—or foolish—to give up yet. After all, we had orders to fulfil. So, we carried on with our little business. We needed more cigarettes, and had no choice but to return to the site after tea when it was getting dark, and take a torch with us.

We managed to get out of our houses at seven p.m. and made our way to the site. Things were much easier at the site with a torch. We had to be very careful when we opened the hole up: there was so much rubble and debris that it was dangerous. We dropped down and, with the aid of our torch, counted the cigarettes: about 40,000 in all. That was great! We should be able to make a fortune!

Stupidly, we hadn't taken a rope and so had to make the precarious climb back up the wall using the footholds we had made. With the aid of the torch, we looked through at our 'bomb.' It really *was* a bomb, a great big grey-coloured bomb with fins at the back. It had gone through the floor and was wedged in what was once a stairwell. There was nothing holding it up, and the slightest movement of the rubble supporting it might release it to fall some eight feet to the concrete floor.

We were really frightened then. We could have so easily been killed while climbing about down there. We had to tell the police and not go back down, because it was just too risky. Trouble was, we would have to admit to everyone we had been there, we would lose our money-making opportunity, and we would get in all sorts of trouble. We collected as many cigarettes as we could carry and walked off home to hide our booty, and try to decide how and when to call the police.

What we didn't know was that two other lads, Frank Pope and Barry Major, had followed us. We never saw them in the dark. They wanted to find where we had got our cigarettes and had overheard us arranging to meet. These two boys watched us as we recovered some more cigarettes, then they waited until we had gone, uncovered our hole, and jumped down into the cellar. They had no torch and only a few matches, which were soon used up. They had seen the cigarettes all right but in their joy over finding them, they hadn't worked out how they were going to get out. As they were trying to climb and jump in the dark, Frank fell, landed awkwardly, and sprained his ankle. They had no light and shouted for help. After a while they realised that no one could hear them. They couldn't climb out and they were stuck until help came, or until morning when they might be able to see better.

Jim and I decided we would do nothing until morning. We would meet up at eight a.m. and go down to the site. If we thought we could, we would rescue a few more 'fags' then call the police and take the consequences. We were both going to wear at least three pairs of pants in an attempt to reduce the pain of the caning that seemed inevitable. I put that thought out of my mind and watched a little TV (black and white, of course) before going to bed.

When Frank and Barry didn't come home, their parents rang round all their friends and then called the police. Officers did what they could and looked everywhere anyone could think of, but no one thought of looking in a bombsite near the school. They came to my house, and my dad woke me to ask if I'd seen them, but I hadn't and it never occurred to me where they might be. I went back to sleep, trying not to dream of canes and the pain they brought.

Promptly at eight, Jim and I met up and went down to the bombsite. As soon as the coast was clear, we went over the fence and moved quickly to the back of the site. To our surprise, our hole was uncovered. We shone a torch down as we heard a faint call for help. In the beam of our torch, we saw two very dirty boys: Barry standing and Frank sitting on the rubble.

"What you doing down there?" I asked them.

"Trying to get out, ain't we?" came the reply.

"You're trying to nick our fags."

"No, we're not. We're just looking round. Anyway, they aren't your fags."

"You must have followed us, you dirty sneaks." (We used to talk like that then!) "The police are looking for you."

"Oh hell, we've been here all night. Frank's hurt his ankle. Help us out."

"Jim and I got out okay. But then, we *are* clever and nimble, not like you two bozos."

"Please?"

"We'll think about it."

They carried on begging us to help them. We told them to wait, and we would get help. As we stood talking to them, Jim shone his torch down on the bomb. It had moved! Frank and Barry's attempts to get out had caused the bomb to shift so that it had slipped further down and hung even more precariously above the cellar floor. We shouted at them to remain still and ran off to get help.

There was a Telephone Box along from the school. We ran there, excitedly rang 999, and asked for the police. The woman who answered sounded doubtful, as if she didn't believe us, but said they would have to check it out. We ran back to school, into the sports hall, and collected one of the long thick ropes that were attached to the ceiling for students to climb. We rushed back over to the site ready to rescue our friends.

Trouble was: what could we fix the rope to? We weren't strong enough to hold it, and everything else was unsafe to fix it to. As we stood there thinking and looking around, two police officers arrived. They shouted at us to come out of the site, but we stood our ground and they came in to us. I thought they were going to drag us away without listening, but we managed to point down to Frank and Barry. Then, having got their attention, we showed them the bomb.

"Bloody hell!" one of them said. He stayed with us while the other one went off to get help and to evacuate the area.

The policeman who stayed let the rope down for the boys to tie round themselves and we helped pull Frank, then Barry up out of their hole. An ambulance arrived and took them off to hospital for treatment and reunion with their parents. We all retreated to a safe distance, which was right round the other side of the school— and then some.

The police called out the Army Bomb Disposal Unit. They attended quite quickly and assessed the situation. They decided it was impossible to safely defuse the bomb, and it couldn't be safely moved, so it would have to be detonated on site.

The bomb was five hundred pounds, and was going to make a mighty big bang and destroy quite a lot of nearby property. The police made sure everyone was safely evacuated from surrounding roads, which they closed off. The school was evacuated and nearby windows boarded up. Then the bomb squad did what they could to contain the blast, and finally detonated the bomb.

It was a wonderful big bang that felt like an earthquake, shaking every building and the ground, smoke and ash filling the air. Jim and I couldn't help thinking that our cigarettes—and the profit they represented—were in there.

Oh well.

When we were allowed back, we went to look at the site. The houses on either side had gone, and where our site had been, there was just a great big hole. Every window on the School's front had been blown out, and debris was spread around despite the efforts to contain the blast.

The neighbours found that the leader of the Council was there, and they soon gathered round and had a real go at him. If he had sorted out the site years ago, this might not have happened. What was he going to do for them now? How long was it going to take to rebuild? Would they be consulted? And many other similar questions.

He promised that those who had lost their homes would be re-housed and everyone would be fully consulted about what to do next. People from the press were there to record his promise. It was, of course, a big story in the local press and made the main evening news on our little black and white TV.

Jim and I were heroes. Our pictures were in the papers, we were interviewed by the local radio, and reporters came to our homes. The next day was Saturday, so we avoided the inevitable trouble at School. We hoped the damage to the School would keep it closed for a while, but it was ready for us by Monday morning. All four of us were back at school, trying to be brave and pretending that we weren't worried.

It wasn't long before we were summoned to go and see the Headmaster. Frank and Barry went in first, while we put our ears to the door and listened. We could hear them getting a good telling off, and then there was the telltale *swish-crack* as they were given the cane: three strokes each.

We trembled in our boots as we waited our turn. We had a little chuckle at Frank and Barry when they came out trying to look as if the cane hadn't hurt. Then in we went. The Head was standing in the study, holding a cane and striking it into his open hand as he stared fiercely at us. I gulped as we awaited our fate.

"If ever anyone deserved a real thrashing, it's you two. You went on the site against school rules, you took cigarettes which didn't belong to you, and you had the temerity to sell them in my school! By my reckoning, that means you deserve six strokes each."

He paused for effect and then continued, "Against that, you raised the alarm and saved two boys and perhaps the whole area, including the children of this school. People will remember the events of the last few days for a long time, and I want them to remember the part children from this school played as positive and good, rather than as a school that produces rule-breaking, money-grabbing, risk-taking young tearaways. Now, as Jesus once said, 'Go thy way and sin no more'."

We didn't need telling twice and went our way, very relieved to have escaped a good hiding.

The Council decided to ask everyone who lived in the area for their views before deciding on a course of action for developing the site. They sent a leaflet round which produced lots of ideas. They held a big meeting in the school sports hall to invite opinions. Almost everyone going into the meeting went past the bomb site, where the deep crater was now filled with water. Presumably, the bomb had fractured a main water pipe.

The water-filled crater looked rather nice and gave the people a good idea. A lake would be lovely, but would look a little strange in the middle of houses. It was suggested at the meeting, and everyone thought it was a really good idea, to extend Queens Park almost down to the road opposite the school, and to incorporate the lake with an island and perhaps with some swans and ducks.

They got to work almost immediately, and within a few months had built a lovely lake over the bomb site in a nice, enlarged park. Everyone agreed it was good use of the site. All the people who lived round about were very happy with it, and, of course, it still looks good today for people to walk round and enjoy.

Rebecca took her thumb out, "Is that a true story, Granddad?"

George smiled. "Well, Rebecca, there *is* a lake in Queens Park, and on a stormy day when the water in the lake is stirred up, if you look closely, they say that you may find a cigarette or two floating on the lake, perhaps some of the forty thousand cigarettes we found that exciting day, long, long ago."

About the Author:

John Bourne lives on the south coast of England with his wife Sandra. He has led a varied life; working in London for the New Zealand High Commission, then spending 18 years in Kent Police, leaving as a sergeant to train for the Christian Ministry in the

Church of England. He was ordained at Canterbury Cathedral in 1991. After a curacy in Maidstone, Kent, he became Vicar of Marden, Kent, and Chaplain of Her Majesty's Prison Blantyre House in 1994.

After nine happy years at Marden, ill health forced early retirement in 2003. By then he had two grown up children, and last year became a grandfather for the first time, another child is due shortly.

In retirement he was able to write. His first book; 'Coppering the Cannon' was written under the pseudonym of James Cannon. In it we meet murder, violence, terrorism, rape, industrial disputes, robbery and public order, and everything else you can think of. Mixing humour and pathos, life and death, success and failure we are taken on a fascinating journey through the eyes of a young policeman in the 1970s.

His second book is a novel; *The Death of Innocence* published as an E-book by Digital Pulp Publishing and available on their web site www.dppstore.com

He is currently working on another novel, and plans a further book on his police service and one about the change from the Police to the Church.

NOSES, TOES, AND ELBOWS
©2006 by Tricia Spencer

"Five, six, seven, eight...."

Shaney sighed and pirouetted to the music for the hundredth or so time in the long afternoon session. But this was no joyfully inspired *Swan Lake*. Her feet hurt, her back screamed, and Jake—not tights and tutus—consumed her thoughts. At fifteen, ballet class no longer held the attraction it used to. Boys did that now. At least: one boy, one *very hot* boy; and Shaney was anxious to escape the class and scoot off to the local Starbucks to meet him for a little sweetened coffee and a lot of sweet snuggles.

"Noses, girls, I need to see those noses."

Six heads dutifully tilted upward, their noses navigating slightly toward the ceiling fluorescents. Ideally, the nose point would give their necks that requisite long-line elegance of the graceful swan, but as her nose elevated, Shaney's thoughts were anything but graceful. Forget swan on a lake, she was thinking swan on a spit. Stuffed and skewered over a licking flame was what the fowl deserved, she mused, for lately she had begun to blame the poor creature for everything. No matter what they danced to, they always had to be swans. Arch this, glide that. It was really starting to prick her nerves.

She was getting just as annoyed with the next stock verbiage she knew would be tumbling out of Miss Gayle's mouth. Her teacher was nothing if not predictable.

"Toes, ladies. Toes to the floor, heels out the door."

"There it is," Shaney moaned under her breath, her imagination conjuring up a vision of an annoying parrot living in Miss Gayle's gullet where it squawked and spouted the same insipid phrases over and over. *Polly want a cracker? Toes to the floor. Polly want a cracker? Heels out the door. Polly want a cracker?*

It was getting so tired.

Shaney watched herself in the mirrored walls, fantasizing about shedding her white swan elegance and becoming a sleek, mean, black swan instead. Thanks to once finding herself on the business end of a wing-flapping chase and a bite that had stung for a week, she'd learned firsthand about black swan temper. Never mind white swan grace, Shaney was ready for a little black swan attitude.

Catching a glimpse of Miss Gayle in the mirror, she eyed the woman's parting lips, and Shaney's own mouth silently mimicked the words she knew were coming.

"Elbows, my swans, gentle the elbows."

Shaney's timing was perfect. Miss Gayle might as well have been a wooden dummy sitting on Shaney's ventriloquist knee. She popped her lips in satisfaction, for she definitely had Miss Gayle pegged. Noses, toes, and elbows. That was Miss Gayle's world. But lately Shaney had begun to believe there had to be more. Maybe it was just that awkward transition of being fifteen going on twenty-one, the age when the Jakes of the world became more important than food or sleep or breathing. Or maybe it was just that she felt worn out so early in life. Ballet was hard. It demanded more of body and soul than most life pursuits and was frequently downright debilitating. And what good was it anyway in the larger scheme of things? The odds of becoming a prima ballerina were about as great as winning the lottery, so why continue with this little girl dream, even if it was the only true dream she'd ever really had? Sure, she'd always wanted to find her prince as the beautiful Odette in *Swan Lake*, or fight for her love as Kitri in *Don Quixote*, but somehow, little by little, the dream had been slipping. The young man ordering her decaf cinnamon latte at that very moment surely played a role in that dream-altering erosion.

She glanced at the wall clock. Just a few more minutes of torture and she would be free. Jake and the sweetly spiced coffee were imminent, and she willed the time to fly as she and five other tortured teen bodies swirled like fluttering snowflakes before contorting themselves into that I'm-a-graceful-swan-floating-on-sparkling-water deep bow that signaled the end.

The end.

Amen and hallelujah. Shaney beelined for the dressing room without waiting for the official "See you tomorrow" from Miss Gayle, only to be stopped cold in her tracks when she heard her name echo in the cavernous studio.

Turning back, she all but stomped her satin-clad feet at the delay, the black swan attitude already starting to rear its ugly little head. Yet, in the end, her voice was respectful, as she knew it would be.

"Yes, Miss Gayle?"

"Shaney, after you change, would you please come back to the studio? I need to talk to you."

The request was met with a decidedly less than enthusiastic response. "But I have to meet someone. Can we talk tomorrow?"

"No, dear. It needs to be today. I'll see you in a few moments."

Miss Gayle didn't wait for an agreement from her star protégé; she just turned on her own satin-clad heel and walked away. She knew Shaney would do as she asked.

Shaney knew it too, and it made her want to smack herself. She was a terrible black swan. She couldn't even stand her ground with one petite woman, let alone have the courage to bite back at her. Resigned, she turned and flew to the dressing room to shower and change, figuring if she cut the shower to thirty seconds, she could still get to Jake before her latte was completely snarky.

Ten minutes later, she stood alone in a studio now eerily stark and hollow without the swish and swirl of a half dozen bodies interpreting the passion of Tchaikovsky or some other long dead virtuoso.

She waited expectantly for Miss Gayle, watching forlornly as the other girls filed from the building to salvage what was left of the afternoon. Suffering minutes crawled by, but her teacher was nowhere to be seen. With only her mirrored reflections for company, Shaney paced and stewed, then paced some more. The clock's second hand throbbed a loud, steady beat in the silent room, mercilessly ticking away her life. And as the time passed ever so agonizingly slowly, her impatience mushroomed until it was downright painful. Finally, she headed for Miss Gayle's office, not wanting to intrude on whatever was delaying her, but not wanting even more to miss her date with the guy who made her heart skip.

Pulling her cell phone from her pocket as she walked to the far end of the studio, she punched the speed dial and waited for Jake to answer. If he did, she didn't know. Just as she reached the office door, it swung open and a pair of gloved hands shot out of nowhere to grab her by the shoulders and yank her into the room. Her cell phone flew from her grip and glided across the polished floor, twirling with great flair, as it did its best imitation of its owner's impassioned recitals.

Shaney cried out, only to have her squeal silenced by one of the leather-encased mitts that had snatched her. She found herself flush up against her attacker, her back to his front, her feet dangling in the air. Scared witless, she didn't even fight; she just hung there like a petrified, captured rabbit, her eyes darting toward Miss Gayle, where she sat stone still in her desk chair. A hideous bruise purpled one of the teacher's cheeks, and the knuckles of her delicate hands blanched white from her iron grip on the chair's mahogany arms.

Shaney felt Miss Gayle's gaze reach out to her even as her instructor visibly forced herself to stillness. Their eyes connected, but neither spoke. Shaney understood the woman's silence, for she, too, hoped that remaining motionless would lessen the palpable fury of the burly men controlling them. Shaney couldn't see the face of her own captor, but the one towering over Miss

Gayle wore a look of blind rage on his ruddy face, his hands clenching and unclenching over and over as if they were milking some invisible cow.

"I'm only going to ask once more, Gayle, where is it?"

The menacing ultimatum sounded like a death threat to Shaney as she watched the giant of a man lean over her tiny instructor and draw back one meaty fist to back up his intimidation.

"I told you, Warren," Miss Gayle swore, tilting her head to look him straight in the eye, "I don't have it. I never had it. I didn't even know Rick had it. Please, don't hurt Shaney. She has nothing to do with any of this. Let her go. Please."

Rick was Miss Gayle's ex-husband. Shaney had seen him once when he'd come to the studio in the middle of class. Miss Gayle had angrily sent him away, and no doubt Shaney was only now learning the reason why.

Miss Gayle's response to the monster towering over her was clearly not the one he wanted. He hit her again. Long auburn hair fell from its dancer bun as her head snapped back and blood spurted from her nose.

Shaney felt the punch as if she—not Miss Gayle—had been its recipient. She fainted.

"What the hell?" The man clutching Shaney to his chest like the prize catch-of-the-day cursed as he felt her go limp in his arms. "The girl's out, Warren," Alan informed his brother as he dumped her onto the floor, grateful to not have to hold her anymore.

Miss Gayle's face contorted with worry as fat tears fell to mix with the blood splaying in an ever-widening swathe over her cheeks and chin. She tried to focus on her student where she lay as still as the dead, but the dance instructor's eyes were swimming and she dared not lift a hand to brush the tears lest Warren break her fingers for the effort.

"For the last time, Gayle, where is the money?"

"I wish I knew. God, I wish I knew," she cried. "Warren, don't you think I'd tell you if I knew? You know I left Rick as soon as I learned about the smuggling. I hated him for having another life I never knew about, and I never got a penny of that money. Not one penny. I wouldn't want it!"

Miss Gayle desperately tried to make Rick's old partners understand even as she damned her ex for apparently double-crossing them and doing God knew what else.

Warren backed up several paces and put his fist through the glass front of a large keepsake case. His anger was too far gone to allow reason any space in his mind. His brain may have known she was telling the truth, but his gut refused to acknowledge it. Stomping back to her, he hauled back once more, and this time the blow knocked her out. Satisfied with his handiwork, he cocked his head and led his brother from the office, closing the door on the two unconscious females. He would deal with them later.

"I'm going to search this place. You go to Gayle's apartment and take it apart. I'll meet you at The Bull Pit after..." Warren paused to look back at the office door, "...after I'm done here."

His meaning was clear to Alan. They weren't going to be able to leave blabbering female lips alive. So be it. Alan didn't care one way or the other. Like his brother, all he wanted was the half million that was his. Unfortunately, the whiny Rick had died before he told them where it was. They should never have gotten involved with the pansy, ballet-loving, good-for-nothing in the first place. In the face of the smallest of tortures, the weasel had just given up the ship and died; worthless dog that he was.

Nodding his agreement, Alan stalked out, and Warren focused on finding the hidden booty. He headed for the dressing room only to be stopped two steps later by a flash of silver. Shaney's cell phone glistened against the mirrored wall where it had violently concluded its sashay across the floor. Warren stalked over, scooped it to his ear, and listened. Dead air. With a grunt, he dropped it to the floor, threw all of his 260 pounds into its demolition, and crushed the potential lifeline with one slam of his heel. Kicking away the debris, he marched on to the dressing room.

In the office, Shaney stirred and opened her eyes. Where was she? What an awful dream she'd had.

Sitting up she spied Miss Gayle slumped sideways in her chair, the teacher's battered head lolling over one back corner, an arm dangling limply to the floor. It wasn't a dream, and reality flooded back in a sickening wave. Shaney's gaze quickly swept the whole room and she swayed with relief as she found the two men gone. Pushing herself to her feet, she headed toward Miss Gayle, but the shattering of glass and the splintering of wood reverberating from beyond the door, ruthlessly dashed any hopeful reprieve. The men were still there. They were just searching the studio for whatever they thought Miss Gayle had.

Swallowing hard, Shaney tried to think. Heaven help her, she could use a little black swan bravery about now.

Moving with the quiet measure of the ballerina she was, she made her way to the phone on Miss Gayle's desk only to stop short when she saw the severed cord sticking from its side. Beside it lay the pulverized remains of what was once Miss Gayle's cell phone. There would be no calling for help.

A low moan snatched Shaney's attention from the useless phones, and she hurried to help the wounded woman sit up. Movement brought a louder cry, and Shaney instinctively put her hand over the dance instructor's mouth to muffle the sound, holding it there for only a second before removing it from the beautiful face now ravaged by giant knuckles. She prayed the men had not heard.

"They're still here, Miss Gayle," she whispered, "out in the studio, tearing it apart. We have to be quiet so they don't come back."

Miss Gayle nodded her understanding, but she knew they would come back no matter what they did—or didn't—find. "I'm so sorry, I..." Grotesquely swollen lips refused to let more words pass.

Shaney shook her head. "It's not your fault. I know it isn't. But what do you think we should do?"

There was no answer. Her teacher had once again slipped into unconsciousness.

"Miss Gayle? Miss Gayle?"

The frantic whispers were to no avail. There was no response, and the tears welled up as Shaney realized just how badly her teacher was hurt. She was scared for herself, but even more so for the woman who had been her mentor for so many years. They had a bond, an undeniable life-altering bond that went beyond teacher and student. They shared desires and passions and dedication, and Shaney could not admire anyone more. But now, if Miss Gayle didn't get medical attention, she would die. Shaney was sure of it.

Alone and miserable, the frightened girl covered her face with her hands and gave in to the tears. She longed to wail to the heavens, but, wisely, wept silently instead. Her fingers felt clammy and foreign against her skin and she wanted to just curl up and wish it all away. If only she could. But she knew that wasn't an option and, to her credit, her meltdown was short lived. The discipline of dance had taught her that control brought results, so she drew a deep breath and sniffed back the tears. She would not give up, not for her sake, and not for Miss Gayle's.

Wiping her cheeks with the back of her hand, she studied the room. At first glance all seemed hopeless. There was only plush furniture and the usual office paraphernalia, some potted plants and flowers, and a myriad of framed and encased mementos. Nothing that screamed *Use me! I'll save you!* The office was lovely and feminine; it wasn't an arsenal.

With desperation hanging over her like a guillotine about to fall, Shaney's gaze landed upon the one thing that had always inspired her past the many aches and pains and missed parties that constituted her life: that glorious painting of Miss Gayle as the beguiling Gizelle. It had been one of her teacher's most famous performances, and she'd been the talk of the ballet world the day of her Gizelle debut, some ten years ago.

Shaney remembered going to the theater as a small girl and being completely captivated by the Cinderella magic of the ballet and the heart stopping beauty that was the prima ballerina. That ballerina had been Miss Gayle. Looking at the painting now,

Shaney felt shame that she had been so close to forgetting the gift she had been given in qualifying for Miss Gayle's class. Truth stared her in the face, forcing her to admit that somewhere along the way she had begun to think of herself more as Jake's girl and less as Shaney the ballerina. She'd been dancing all her life, pirouetting and jetéing her way to the fulfillment of a dream. She felt horrible that she had, even for a moment, considered quitting. She wasn't a quitter. She may be crazy for Jake, but ballet was who she was.

Leaning both hands on the desk, Shaney squeezed her eyes shut and prayed for a miracle. There had to be a way to survive. "I just have to find it," she ordered herself in a whisper. "I can do this."

Mere seconds later, she opened her eyes and found her hoped-for miracle staring right back at her in bold black and white. There, atop a pile of correspondence, was a crisp white letter bearing her name. *This* was why Miss Gayle had wanted to talk to her. Her heart hammered her ribs as she read the incredible words.

After having reviewed the tapes you submitted, and with great respect for your recommendation, we will be honored to give consideration to Miss Shaney Masser for the role of Clara in this season's touring company of the Nutcracker. We look forward to meeting her.

The letter bore the seal of the American Ballet Theater. She was going to audition for the lead in The Nutcracker! Shaney could barely draw breath, and it wasn't from debilitating fear; it was from standing just a toe away from her dreams. Dancing almost since she was old enough to know she had feet, she had envisioned her first big audition, rehearsing in her mind, so many times in so many ways, that memorable inaugural step onto a grand stage. Her imagination took flight, and she felt joy bubble up and shove the terror of the moment to the farthest corner of her thoughts.

She grabbed the letter and held it to her chest and as she lifted her gaze once more to the portrait of Miss Gayle, her teacher's mantra began to drum a spirited rhythm into Shaney's brain. Like the clacking of a train as it picks up speed, the words pulsed through her, again and again and again.

Noses, toes, and elbows.

Noses, toes, and elbows.

Noses, toes, and elbows.

The words just kept pummeling her, lifting her, giving her purpose. All her life, Shaney had wanted this, and she wasn't going to lose it now, not to some low-life crooks who thought slugging a woman was all in a day's work.

With solemn reverence, she returned the precious letter to the desk and quietly moved around the office, searching for something—*anything*—that might save them. There were no windows for escape, and going out the door and walking right into the two men would be suicide. It had to be something else.

The very specific destructive sounds now coming from the studio could mean only one thing. The men were ripping the mirrors from the walls looking for hidden secrets that Shaney was sure weren't even there. She stopped to listen, straining to hear them talk, praying that when they finished they might just leave. But there was no conversation, and to Shaney's trained musical ear, something else—or the lack of it—was just as telling. There were no simultaneous crashes, or even conflicting crashes. It was just one explosion at a time, one single solitary event. Could it be? Could there be only one of the men out there now? She held her breath and waited, but not a word was uttered and there was only the slap of one set of footsteps on the hardwood floor as the man made his way around the room. Hope exploded in her belly. One of them was gone! The realization that two foes had been whittled to one gave wings to Shaney's determination.

Accepting that escape was out of the question, she had to find a weapon. Her eyes systematically roamed from wall to wall as her mind rapidly judged each object's lethal potential. When she came to the vintage drum major mace displayed in a case that now bore a broken glass front, she knew she'd found her armament. The rare vintage *Music Man* keepsake would surely do the trick, but Shaney had to figure out how to get it out of its enclosure without making a sound.

Darting to the loveseat by the door, she snatched one of the velvety throw pillows resting there. The daintily-flowered cushion was unzipped and deprived of its stuffing in one fell swoop as she made her way back to negotiate the broken glass of the case.

She knew she had to be careful and silent. Wearing the pillowcase as a glove, she reached through the fist-sized gap, flinching as shards of glass dislodged and sprinkled her feet as they fell to the carpeted floor.

Shaney grabbed the mace and was grateful to find it was not as heavy as it looked. But the jagged hole in the glass was not in the right spot to get the four-foot long baton through it. She would have to break the glass even more. Surely, she couldn't do that without the man on the other side of the door hearing the outcome.

There was no choice. The demolition of the studio sounded ever closer, and time was not on her side. He would finish soon and come for them.

She withdrew her hand and dashed back to the loveseat for another pillow. Returning as fast as her feet would fly, she laid the plump cushion against the outside of the glass with her left hand and sent her right hand through the opening to wrap the empty pillowcase around the end of the drum major's staff. Satisfied she'd done all she could to ensure the secrecy of her actions, she closed her eyes—as if doing so would bring the silence she prayed for—and tapped the glass from the inside with the baton's cloth sheathed head. It worked. The glass shattered, but pillow protection notwithstanding, the result wasn't the least bit silent.

The muffled sound of the exploding glass sounded like a cannon boom to Shaney and her head jerked toward the door, expecting the worst. With a sick pit in her stomach, her expectations were met. The annihilation beyond the door abruptly halted and a few seconds of quiet were followed by the sound of quickened footsteps heading her way.

Silence no longer mattered and Shaney yanked the mace from its enclosure, sending glass flying every which way in the process. Lifting the baton high before her with both hands, she leaped over the litter of broken glass, sprang onto the loveseat, and balanced herself on the top of the overstuffed back. It was only seconds before the office door blew open at the hand of the enemy.

Without hesitation, Shaney swung. The carved eagle on the head of the mace caught the man square on the fat of his nose, sending him reeling backwards to trip over his own feet and crash to the floor. She knew it wouldn't be enough.

Flying from the sofa back, she landed in the doorway and swung the baton downward. *Chop! Chop! Chop!* Like an axe man chewing through a stump, she swung over and over, turning that bloodied nose to pulp, until the man's eyes fluttered closed and he stilled.

Shaney thought she was going to be sick but hesitated only a heartbeat before throwing down her weapon and racing a path through broken mirrors and unidentifiable debris to the dressing room, returning quickly with her hands full of leggings. Picking up the baton, she shoved it under the man's back until it stuck out from both sides of his waist like the supporting beam of a scarecrow's cross. Tending first one side, then the other, she crooked his elbows around the mace and tied them to it with the leggings she had grabbed from the mutilated dressing room lockers. Her knots were tight and the man's arms were fixed solid against the inflexible wood.

Moving swiftly, as if she had rehearsed and performed this particular tragedy a thousand times before, Shaney turned to his feet and looped the rest of the leggings around his boots. An eerie moan from the fallen brute told her he was coming to, and she tied and knotted like a demon, finishing just as his eyes popped open.

His bellow of pain and fury threatened to peel her from her skin, but she had done her work well. He could do no more than flop about like a beached whale, the head of the mace banging against the wooden floor with each desperate pitch of his body, his feet countering with whacks of their own as they tried to find a way to erect their owner. The rapid-fire cadence of the mace thumps and the feet whacks were as frantic and hopeless as the flapping wings of a trapped bird, only this was no bird.

Backing up until she felt the office doorjamb at her back, Shaney shivered with the realization of what she'd done. The man was a giant, and she had felled him. The impact of her actions took its toll and she began to melt into a heap as her legs turned to spaghetti beneath her. Slithering down the doorjamb in slow motion, she stared at the bull of a man flopping and screaming where swans had floated, and she knew one thing: she knew she'd never again think about giving up her dream.

With a crash, the studio door burst open and two policemen charged in, guns drawn, Jake hot on their heels. Unable to raise Shaney on her cell after her call had come in, Jake had quickly progressed from worry to absolute belief that something was terribly wrong. He'd called 911, and then raced over to the studio where he and the arriving officers were welcomed by anguished bellows rattling the rafters.

The sight that met the rescuers as they barreled through the door was one the police would be talking about for years to come. A wisp of a girl hunkered down in the doorway without a mark on her, and on the floor, a giant thug with a nose of minced meat, trussed up with pale pink and baby blue bows at his feet and elbows, rolling and squalling like a stuck pig.

"Shaney!"

Jake was beside her in an instant, scooping her into protective arms.

"Miss Gayle...help her."

Jake looked up but one of the police officers was already on his radio calling for the paramedics.

"Shaney, are you hurt? What happened?"

Shaney looked at Jake and suddenly she knew she really was all right and Miss Gayle was going to be saved. Worry slid from her face as if it had never belonged there and a bright smile took its place. She wanted to tell Jake all about what had happened, but all that came out was, "I'm going to audition for the Nutcracker!"

Jake's look of utter confusion made Shaney laugh. She would tell him everything in due course, but for now she just wanted to think about the joy of one brief, amazing, letter.

One of the cops bent over Warren to make sure the flailing man was secure. Not that he needed to, for the bound-up crook was as useless as a landlocked trout. Satisfied the man wasn't going anywhere, the officer stood and walked over to Jake and Shaney, still shaking his head at the wonder of it all. Both teens rose to their feet as the officer voiced the burning question.

"I have to ask one thing first, young lady. How on earth did you do all of this?"

Sirens wailed as back-up officers and paramedics bolted into the studio, and the budding ballerina swan looked toward the vile man she'd bested. A couple of newly arrived cops hauled the criminal to his feet and traded the leggings for handcuffs. He was still howling like a banshee.

Dismissing him as worthless of further consideration, Shaney's gaze swiveled to look through the office door to where Miss Gayle sat; awake now, holding a tissue to her battered face. Slowly Shaney brought her fingertips to her lips and blew her teacher a kiss before turning to the officer, a look of calm resolve on her face.

"Noses, toes, and elbows, sir," she answered matter-of-factly, "noses, toes, and elbows."

That Christmas the reviews would herald the arrival of a new star and proclaim that those who'd had the good fortune of witnessing Shaney Masser's debut as Clara would remember it for a lifetime. A new prima ballerina, with an uncanny and masterful command of the art, was born.

About the author:

Tricia Spencer has been nationally recognized for her work in songwriting, vocal performance, and merchandising, as well as nonfiction and fiction writing.

As an author, she received the Best Nonfiction Book award for "Tips, The Server's Guide to Bringing Home the Bacon—the Customer Speaks!" from the prestigious Southwest Writers International Manuscript Competition. "Tips..." was published in 2002 and has become a training manual for restaurants around the country. Her short story, "Deviled Eggs" was a winner in both the L. Ron Hubbard Writers of the Future Competition for Science Fiction and CrossQuarter Publishing's Paul B. Duquette Memorial Short Science Fiction Contest. "Deviled Eggs" is published in "CrossTime", the 2002 science fiction anthology featuring the winners of the CrossQuarter competition. Her short story, "Miracle Man" was a winner in the 2005 Cloak and Dagger Mystery Writing Contest where the finalists were judged by renowned mystery author Jeremiah Healy. She is listed in "Who's Who of American Women", "Who's Who of Emerging Leaders", "Who's Who in The West", and "Who's Who in The World".

Tricia's life pursuits reflect her philosophy that variety is truly the spice of life. From food service, to touring with the International Company of Up With People, to creating and marketing her own line of wedding accessories, to author, with a world of diverse creative pursuits in between, Tricia has reveled in the highs and lows of self-evolution and in the myriad of endeavors life has to offer.

Born and raised in Central Illinois, she and her husband, Mark, now live in Southern California where they share their home with all manner of furry and feathered creatures. They also share a passion for the simple pleasures of life, like sharing a romantic dinner or reading a good book.

MOTHER'S DAY
©2006 by Julia Halprin Jackson

I'm terrified.

My sixty-year-old mother is giving birth to my daughter.

I have always seen her as Donna Reed high on marijuana. She always wore aprons, skirts and dresses, and the occasional petticoat. She was a fabulous cook. Mother was a professional botanist and gardener. There were flowers everywhere.

Mother was always beautiful. After sixty years, her body changed gradually and the wrinkles in her cheeks, elbows, and knees seemed flawlessly natural. She has the same long curved legs, the same callused hands, the same soft braids. Never before has she seemed so colorful. I am always used to seeing her long and brown between rows of vibrant flowers. Now she is the flower surrounded by a sea of tubes and machines, monitors and lights, doctors and nurses all so vanilla gray. She carries my baby. My baby will travel the same path that I have, and that's what frightens me.

Seven days. I was a mother for seven glorious days. When he was born, I began reading in color. Nathan says one in 25,000 people live with synesthesia—this crossing over of senses like tangled telephone wires, brains processing multiple messages at once, a virtual party line. Elias lay so quietly in my arms, unusually quiet, blissfully quiet, peacefully quiet. His body was every color, his breathing so charmed. After I gave birth, I wrote my first poem. The words were on fire.

After Mother moved, Dad and I were left in that old house alone. All the flowers died. The house grew dank and gray without the hanging plants and daily bouquets. She would pick me up after school every day and take me with her to her greenhouse. Growing up, I never believed in photosynthesis because it was clear that plants only grew when she asked them to. She would bend over the African violets or the orange cosmos and whisper to them, and by the time she stood up they would all turn their petals to the roof. I was convinced that she breathed only their oxygen and they only her carbon dioxide.

She made me daisy crowns and let me keep the sow bugs as pets. They meant little to me at fourteen, and before long, my heart hardened like the flowers on Dad's windowsill, color fading but the smell lingering.

Each year on my birthday she planted a new rosebush in our yard. By my fourteenth birthday our yard was awash in flowers, spilling out of pots and creeping across the stone path. The year she moved, the roses changed color—no longer a salmon pink, they deepened to a dark, fiery red.

After Elias' death, the world had never seemed so devoid of color. Our house was a false pink, my office a dank gray. I ran so many red lights, Nathan remarked I must be colorblind. Noise faded too: all I could hear was my heartbeat—pathetically, unremarkably alone. My arms felt so empty, my breasts so heavy. They tugged my heart downward, lowered my center of gravity so it felt better to crawl on the ground than it did to stand up tall.

Mother came to our house every day for a year. I told her I didn't want nor need her to, and she smiled and brushed my hair while potato leek soup simmered on our childproofed stove. She always brought me flowers and they were always white.

I always preferred reason to poetry, fact to allegory. I liked things explained. This situation, this experience, this existence, was altogether too mysterious for me. But even biology lies. What else could an orphaned mother think? Mother of a dead boy, daughter to a stoned Donna Reed. We had planned the pregnancy to every minute detail. His hands were so small. We did everything right. Reason died in my arms.

Is it still dead?

It had been four years. My law practice was doing well. We finally took that mountain biking trip to the Rocky Mountains. We were remembering the act of laughter. When Elias died, a part of my womb died, too. We lost our child and we lost all future children as well.

Then one day, Mother sent us a newspaper clipping from an online Israeli news source. The headline read *64-year-old Woman Gives Birth to Healthy Baby Boy*. The mother and her husband, who live in Tel Aviv, had been using fertility treatments for over twenty years when they finally conceived with the aid of *in vitro* fertilization. Apparently, they had to lie about their age in order to be considered for the *in vitro* program. The mother was admitted to the high-risk pregnancy unit in her third month, where she was closely monitored until the birth of her son.

"We do not recommend *in vitro* fertilizations for older mothers due to the health risk it poses to women," was all the doctor had to say. The article did not mention what these health risks were, but it did go on to say that the happy couple was overjoyed to finally be parents.

I turned the paper over, but the story went no further. Curious. Mother habitually sent me clippings and stories from the paper, but this was different. It seemed she was trying to suggest something. Nathan and I had already looked into *in vitro* fertilization. The process pinned all of our desperate desires to the Russian roulette of lab tubes and a deflating wallet. We had the money, yes, but Dr. Noelle had already proven to us that there was no medical way for me to bear children. We considered finding a surrogate mother, but tiptoed shyly away from that. What greater decision in our life could we make? We were shopping for child-bearers of our own blood, the most crucial substitutes we would ever need.

Sixty-four-years old.... What was Mother implying? That I still had time?

At the bottom of the article I saw where she had written in her unmistakable fine print: *Life is painful. Suffering is optional. –* *Sylvia Boorstein.*

As if we were given a choice.

After I received Mother's letter in the mail, I decided to give her a call. I don't chat much; usually when I call someone there is some practical purpose. We rarely talked anyway. Mother preferred face-to-face conversations and she took any opportunity to stop by and critique my front garden or offer recipe suggestions. I felt quite foreign picking up the phone. I even had to look up her number in my phone book.

She picked it up on the third ring.

"Mother?"

"Why, hello dear! What a pleasant surprise!" She chatted gaily for a moment about the flower arrangement in her living room. Narcissus, she said, and some violets.

"Mother, a 64-year-old Israeli woman gave birth," I said shortly, not sure where to start. She clucked softly.

"Why is it you never call me 'Mom'?"

"Mother, why did you send me this article?"

She sighed briefly. I could hear her washing out a vase in the sink. "Well, it's a spectacular feat, really. How wonderful it must be to produce life at the end of another...tremendous, if you ask me." She was now scrubbing the glass vase. Her voice fell like the water: natural, even, practiced.

"How tremendous."

"Indeed. Do you know that Agnes and I almost had a child?" The stool I had been sitting on suddenly felt too tall. Was I shrinking? Mother had not talked about her former partner since Agnes' death two years before.

"I didn't know, Mother."

"She was a kindergarten teacher, as you may remember. She loved children. She loved you. I always wanted to have another child." The water was silent.

"Was I not enough?"

"You were perfectly enough, my dear. I loved you. I was full of love—my love for you spilled into my love for flowers, and my love for food, and my love for community. I had so much to share."

"And so, you shared it with Agnes."

"Well, yes. Your father treated me well, and I loved him for his love for you. But Agnes was more. She was compassion, she was joy, she was curiosity. And she wanted so much to share this world with a child. *Her* child."

Agnes was the woman who took my mother away from me.

"And so...?"

"And so, we considered all options. We could have adopted, I guess, but I told her how there is no feeling more triumphant than that of a woman holding her newborn child. I told her what it feels like to feed a child with one's own body, what it sounds like when you awake in the morning and there is a new body breathing in the room. And how satisfying it is to watch this small person as she learns to move, trains her tongue to her own language, asks questions that no adult can answer. Agnes saw what you meant to me, and she wanted it, too."

My body was empty. Any blood I had left rushed to my feet. I felt like stomping.

"Mother, that's what *I* want." I began to cry.

She was quiet. "I know."

She had been in and out of the hospital for several months. The irony never failed me: we were willing to spend thousands of dollars on complicated medical procedures and several months in and out of the hospital, and yet we were relying on the physical and emotional strength of a woman starting her seventh decade, a woman I had trained myself not to trust. What was it that compelled us to believe in her? My shrink was certainly confused. My mother had snuck into our world and transformed it. Again.

Nathan quit his job at the newspaper. He took his reporter's journal to the maternity unit every morning, where he interviewed every willing *in vitro* parent he could find. I remember one evening when I woke up to the feeling of a ghost child in my belly. I walked downstairs and found Nathan asleep on the easy chair before the fireplace, pen in hand. I kneeled down before him and peered across the paper.

Factors that affect fertilization of in vitro egg:
FSH (Follicle Stimulating Hormone) level
Previous births, fertility problems
Age

Possible risks to the mother:
Gestational diabetes
Hypertension
Cardiovascular complications
(Chance of multiple fertilization?)
Complications related to caesarian section

Possible risks to the child:

His pen had fallen here, leaving a dark blue well of ink on the page. Nathan, who wrote me the most beautiful love poems while we were in college but never once took a biology class, was poring over medical journals and Xeroxed microfilm stories from the library. I saw a stack of mimeographed sheets underneath the rocking chair. His curly hair was matted against his forehead just so, drool forming on his lower lip.

During my pregnancy, he wrote one hundred sonnets for Elias. After the birth, Nathan hardly spoke. Every day he would lie in bed with this tiny boy lying motionlessly beside him, kissing Elias' forehead and taking notes. For months afterward, I would find fragments of poems tucked behind dinner plates or in the pockets of old jeans.

My monarch boy, he always used to write. *Wing-swept smile and the most powerful little arms in the world—they caught me when I fell.*

Nathan's nose twitched in his sleep. He snored sometimes, but on this night his nose emitted a thin, tinny whistle. And those little hollows underneath his eyes—small caverns, really—that sank every time he lowered his gaze. Our boy could fit in those eyes.

He looked up, startled, and wiped the drool from his mouth. "Was I snoring?"

"No, better—you were whistling."

He smiled and straightened in his chair. "Must've fallen asleep." He looked at his watch. It was a little past four. "I should get to bed. Your mother has another appointment at the Prenatal Unit in four hours." He started to organize his books and papers.

"Nathan?" He looked up suddenly. "Do you trust her?" I asked.

He jumped slightly. He examined me slowly, as he used to examine the subjects of his stories, as he used to examine his child. I could tell he was writing something in his head.

"I trust *us*." His hand appeared suddenly on my belly. I stared at him hard, trying to read his next words. How was he so convinced?

"Your mother gave birth to you, and you turned out all right." He managed a weak laugh. I didn't smile. Those cavernous eyes dug craters in his cheeks.

"My mother gave birth to me and I gave birth to a doomed boy. My mother gave birth to me and I can barely stand at the end of the day because all I can think about is my baby, *our* baby, the baby I will never have. My mother gave birth to a lawyer who is paid to divide up families. Nathan, there are people in this world who can have as many children as they want! There are people in this world who can give their children everything! And then they come to me to see which last name the kid gets stuck with, or if the PlayStation should stay at mom's house or dad's. PlayStation! My mother thinks PlayStation is the new-and-improved Play Dough.

"My mother, who has never owned a television, has already raised her own child. My mother, the goddess, my mother, the queer—she *already* had a child! And now she can look back on her long life and say that she picked up on the things that her daughter dropped off. My mother..."

"...will be a grandmother soon." The caverns were gone. Nathan's face was pure granite. "Again."

My breath caught. We looked at each other for a moment, and then watched as the final flame in the fireplace flickered and died. The room was quiet.

"I keep waiting for Elias to catch me," I whispered. "But I can't stop falling."

We had a birthday party the day the cells were officially fertilized. Mother came home from the clinic and brought her new gynecologist Dr. Grant. Nathan baked bread. I made some origami paper cranes. My next-door neighbor Lesley told me that paper cranes bring luck. I didn't think I believed in luck anymore, but then Nathan pointed out that paper cranes were really just three-dimensional poems, and I thought Elias would have liked them hung above his bed.

I don't really throw parties. Growing up, Mother would invite all the girls in my classes to our house for tea in the garden. She would serve us all in that sea foam green apron and the girls were always charmed. On my twenty-first birthday, Mother sent me a game of Twister and two bottles of champagne. The accompanying note read: "All you need now is someone to play with."

I would have had someone to play with, had she never left Dad for Agnes, or if she and Agnes had had a child. I must have been in college, busy writing my thesis on Earl Warren, when Mother and Agnes were visiting a fertility clinic. It's a good thing I rarely came home for school breaks, or else I might have wandered into a pink playpen or twisted my ankle on a toy horse.

When I did come home it was usually to Dad's old Victorian house, the white one with ivy and the dead rose garden in the front yard. What would that old man have said if I had arrived home Christmas break with a half-sibling? He might have had that coronary a few years earlier....

Nathan's bread warmed on the stove while I finished the origami. Mother loved them. She loved things she could hold in her hands. I wondered what it would be like for her: holding a baby in her hands for the first time in thirty years. I felt suddenly like the baby, cupped between those bronze arms and dependent on her every breath. Each breath both sustained and weakened me.

I kept the origami on the windowsill throughout the pregnancy. Sometimes, in the early morning, I thought I heard tapping on the window. Every time it was the same: I'd walk down the stairs, sweep the hair out of my face, peer outside to the dawning moon low on the horizon, and look for birds. There were never birds in our backyard, not unless Mother had come by to water the hollyhocks. That's when the hummingbirds would come. During the pregnancy, Mother lived mostly on that hospital cot at the clinic, and the hummingbirds stayed away. The only thing tapping on our windowsill was the paper beaks of cranes.

At our fertilization celebration, I served champagne. Mother drank apple cider. Nathan made a toast.

"To our family!" he said. It sounded less peculiar when he said it.

"To your family!" said Dr. Grant.

"To the young parents," said Mother. She drank slowly. I drank fast.

Later that evening, Mother approached me in the hallway as she prepared to leave. "I'm sorry I forgot Twister," she said.

I was on my third glass of champagne and was feeling pink. "I think what we're really playing is Clue."

"Perhaps, but you know what?"

I never knew what. When was she going to see that? "What?"

"I think this time you'll have someone to play with."

It's Saturday, May 29, ten in the morning. The C-section is scheduled for eleven-thirty. I am sitting in Mother's room with her. How does she always look at peace?

"My body finally feels useful," she says. She convinced the orderly to hang a bird feeder outside her window so she could watch the hummingbirds, and now two of them hover.

"You're a gardener," I remind her. "Your body has always been useful."

The hummingbirds have pink throats and red wings.

"Your father always used to say that my skin felt like the underbelly of a crab." She rubs her belly slowly in a circular pattern. "He thought I had a shell."

"Dad always was the king of backhanded compliments."

"You think I'm a crab, too." Her thumb plays with her navel.

"I never said that."

"You think my arms are pincers." She glances at her elbows. "Otherwise you wouldn't be so afraid to touch me."

"I'm trying to protect the baby..."

"You're trying to protect yourself." The hummingbirds have flown away. She turns her gaze to me.

Dr. Grant knocks on the door, clipboard tucked under his arm. "Morning, ladies!"

Mother says "Good morning, Dr. Grant," without taking her eyes off me.

"How're you feeling, Mom?"

"Fine," we both say too quickly.

Dr. Grant raises his eyebrows. He stops to take Mother's pulse. "In one hour, *your* job will be over," he says to Mother. He jots down her blood pressure, then turns to me. "But *your* job will be just beginning. You both must be so excited."

"I think I'll miss being pregnant," Mother says.

Dr. Grant laughs. "Now *that's* not something I usually hear!"

"It's been thirty years since I've felt this full."

Dr. Grant leans across the cot and pats her gently on the shoulder. "You'll soon be a grandmother," he reminds her. "There are few feelings more full than that of a grandmother holding her grandchild. I should know: I'm a grandfather myself." Mother reflects his smile and he picks up his clipboard. "Besides, as a grandmother you'll be able to watch the child grow without even having to change diapers in the middle of the night."

"When she was a baby, I would change her outside," Mother smiles at me. "In the rose garden, in the moonlight."

"I suppose that would help the smell," Dr. Grant replies. He chuckles at his own joke and checks his watch again. "Best rest up, you two, because we've got a big day ahead!" He pats us both on the shoulder again and walks out into the hall.

Mother looks down at her hard belly. "We've got a big *life* ahead," she says and turns to me. "What do you think, dear? Will she be an astrophysicist or an international diplomat? Either way, she'll need to go to Harvard."

"She'll be a baby," I say. "That's all that matters."

We both stare outside the window for several minutes. I can see the sun climbing in the sky, feel the air as it enters my nostrils. How incredible it would be to remember one's first breath. I wonder if she will yell as all the other babies in the ward have, or if she will be quiet like Elias. I wonder if Dr. Grant will place the baby immediately in Mother's arms, as they do in made-for-TV movies, or if he will turn and see me sitting here on this hard chair next to the bed, body frozen. Where will Nathan be? Beside me, of course, with his little reporter's notebook, scribbling furiously. And Mother...it is unusual to think of her body so exposed, so vulnerable, even though we have been talking about the C-section for months. She'll be blooming.

"I love her already." Mother reaches across to hold my hand. "Just as I love you." Her eyes are full like her womb.

"You're no crab," I say, my hand limp and cold in hers. "Crabs don't give birth the way humans do." Her eyes well. I reach my hand gingerly across her face to brush her sterling hair back behind her ears. "I—you—she will be beautiful."

"Yes, she will."

We turn to the window, where the hummingbirds are hiding.

Eleven thirty-two. Mother's sweating like she does in the

garden. Dr. Grant and two other surgeons are hovering around her with scalpels like fine silver trowels, unearthing our baby. Nathan is holding my hand and hiccupping nervously. He already drank two liters of mineral water and his hands are clammy like the condensation on the bottle. Mother looks doped.

"Nothing hurts," she says, although her eyebrows jerk involuntarily. I notice her knuckles are white, her skin so pale. She looks old, almost inhuman.

She grabs my hand. She keeps pulling me closer, close enough to smell that same old smell like the scent of a fresh-cut tomato, ripe and raw and red. Was she always this grotesque? Is this what I looked like the day Elias was born?

"For you," she whispers.

I'm still staring at her eyes when the squealing starts. Nathan pulls me away and we turn to her, that radiant blur in Dr. Grant's gloves, wailing and singing all at once. The surgeons rush to cut the umbilical cord, just as they cut Elias', just as they separated me and Mother. Dr. Grant wraps a small blanket around her and he walks to our side of the bed, where Nathan and I are already standing, expectant.

"Your daughter," he says, extending the quivering bundle.

Nathan and I hold her together and all I can see are those little black eyes. We watch, speechless, as she moves her arms and legs for the first time. The rest of the room falls away, unimportant. Those knees! I've never seen prettier knees. She's unblemished, soft and still moist from Mother's body. Nathan reaches out a finger and gingerly traces the line from her knee to her toes. His index finger is the same length as her calf.

"Our daughter," he says under his breath. His tears drop on her toes as she continues to wail. I can't concentrate because I can feel her heart beating through the thin blanket. She looks so breakable. She looks like Elias, but she yells louder.

Nathan and I are standing immobile in the middle of the room, our backs to Mother. It's funny how a baby only twenty inches long can become the largest person in the room. Her eyes swallow us whole.

Dr. Grant is busying himself behind us when we turn to see Mother nodding slowly in bed. She looks cold, abandoned, arms empty. I'm afraid to move from this spot and I don't want to see this little girl leave my chest. Nathan nudges me toward Mother. We walk to her bedside and I sit down carefully beside her.

"What an effort!" Nathan says. "Congratulations! You're a grandmother!" He smiles, and Mother inclines her head sage-like, as if granting us something. He turns to me, with my arms wrapped protectively around my little girl, locked into place. Gently he reaches out to take her from me. My arms resist. I gave Elias to the doctors and they held him more than I did.

"Honey, let Mother see the baby," he says to my eyes. "The baby she just delivered," he reminds me, "for us." My arms dissolve and he kisses me on the cheek, cradling the baby in his arms as he turns to Mother.

I'm empty. I don't ever want to be empty again.

Our baby is in *her* arms now, and she stops wailing. The room is eerily quiet. Mother moves her chest just so back and forth while tears draw jagged lines down her leathered cheeks. The baby is spellbound.

"How tremendous it is to start one life at the end of another..." Mother's voice trails off as she kisses our girl's forehead. "How tremendous..."

Nathan smiles and squeezes my hand. I want my baby to scream, to move, to make her presence known. I want the world to know that I have a healthy baby girl. I don't want her to be like Elias. I want her out of Mother's arms.

I reach out suddenly. My arms are drawn to my girl like magnets. I can't help it. She's too quiet. This isn't right.

Mother looks up, but she isn't startled. Instead, she lifts her arms without letting go of the baby, making room for my arms under her own. My arms lock around my daughter, the left under her thin shoulders and the right under her shining legs. My face is inches from Mother's.

Nathan says nothing. Instead he strokes the back of my thigh tenderly.

For a few minutes we sit like this: mother, daughter, and granddaughter in one tightly-wrapped bundle. I've never been so close to Mother's face. Even as I child I never let her kiss me. The wrinkles along her eyes extend out like feathers. She smells like earth.

"Congratulations," she breathes.

Our arms loosen together, and my girl rocks gently between us as I pull her slowly away.

About the Author:

Julia Halprin Jackson is a senior literature major and Spanish minor at the College of Creative Studies (CCS) at the University of California in Santa Barbara. She works as a writing tutor at UCSB's Campus Learning Assisted Services program and as a teaching assistant at CCS' Art Institute for kids. She believes in quality books, quality music, quality people, and quality thought.

WHAT COULD HAVE BEEN
©2006 by Karin B. Schlenker

It started with a discussion about angels. He believed they were human. Essentially, anybody could become an angel after they died. In his version they didn't have wings and so it reminded me of that sappy, but lovable Christmas movie "It's a Wonderful Life." Surprisingly, he didn't even mention the movie. As a matter of fact, he wanted to let the entire discussion go, but I persisted in keeping it alive. Somehow it seemed important to me, but I didn't know why at the time.

I believed that angels were a completely different entity from us, not human at all. I insisted that in the whole scheme of things, even though angels were supposed to have been created below man, I didn't think they were given a very fair deal since *we* were the ones who allegedly screwed up. In essence, I thought they were actually above us, even though they may have been originally created to serve man. Yet, I also knew that angels were most likely envious of us because we had free will and could make our own choices. I don't even pretend to know who created them and us— your guess is as good as mine.

After explaining my theory, his response was "You think entirely too much about these things. I was just trying to start a conversation with you. I don't even know if I believe in angels, especially the way that you describe them, but I'll keep it in mind if I ever come across one."

At least I gave him something to think about. We decided to

resolve the argument by taking a walk in the woods. It was a beautiful fall day, and we walked together quietly, soaking in the colors. The weather was perfect: one of those brisk days that make you want to jump in the next big pile of leaves you see. But we just walked, silent, each keeping our own thoughts to ourselves. I was basking in the beauty of the fall day, trying to decide which color I liked best, when suddenly he turned to me, a serious expression on his face. At that moment, I studied his face deeply. Even though I had seen it countless times before, I noticed for the first time that his brown eyes were his best feature. They were friendly eyes, but it was his thick eyelashes that were the most noticeable. How envious I was of those eyelashes. I would never have to use mascara!

"I quit my job today," he said, looking to see if I would be shocked. He had talked about quitting his job before, but never quite had the nerve to do it, since he was so paranoid about where his next dollar would come from. I wasn't shocked, but I *was* a bit surprised, so I asked him what he was going to do now.

"Oh, I don't know. Maybe I'll take up writing and become a famous author. Maybe I'll sell everything and travel. Or I could just become a bum and live in the streets. I don't know what I'll do, but I knew I couldn't work there anymore. I couldn't go there day in and day out doing something that was totally worthless. Here I am almost forty and I've done nothing with my life."

Even after I reminded him that most of us were in the same situation, he continued, "I've always wanted to write. I feel restless, like I'm missing out on something. I can't go on like this. Who knows, maybe I'll even write a story about angels."

So, in spite of my protests, he began his illustrious writing career. He got up early every morning, made coffee, and sat at the computer, seemingly producing page after page of writing. He lived off his credit card and the generosity of friends, so money wasn't an issue. Sometimes I would bring him a bagel with cream cheese or a croissant. Occasionally, he would take a break and eat, but usually he would just sit there for hours and ignore everything else, merrily typing away on his computer. He told me he was having success, but refused to show me anything. He wanted to be sure it was perfect before I saw it.

Finally, after several weeks of working diligently, he decided his work was good enough to show me.

What I read was not what I had expected. It was a story about when we went to an Indian restaurant on Sixth Street. While waiting for our food, I observed several mice scurrying around on the floor. Instead of leaving after I pointed them out to him, we watched the mice as they sat below our table and ate their dinner as we ate ours. Before we knew it, we were making up stories about them. We gave them names, discussed which colleges they may have graduated from, what majors they had, and how proud their parents must be since they were the family's first college graduates. What was even more amazing, now that I look back at it, is that we ordered food and actually ate it despite the mice.

I couldn't believe he made a story out of that adventure, but he did. I doubted very much that anyone would be interested in a story about mice, but to my surprise it didn't take long until he found a buyer. I honestly believed his next story would be about the Empire State Building-sized cockroaches we saw in that same restaurant's bathroom that day. We celebrated his sale by eating at an expensive restaurant without mice or cockroaches.

The next story was a true one about a couple who cared about each other, but couldn't live together because he was allergic to cats. I was a cat lover, and had at least four cats at any given time. Whenever he came over, he would have to take an allergy pill to handle it. The one time I witnessed him having an asthma attack was extremely frightening, so I knew we could never have animals. We came to the conclusion that the only way we could live together and not get rid of the cats was to get them their own apartment.

His story was about having an apartment solely for the cats. As a matter of fact, it was about a society where it was law that all pets must have their own residence and must be treated with reverence and respect; unlike our own society where we still have a long way to go in such matters. I must say I found the story quite imaginative and it almost had me convinced I should go ahead and get my cats their own place and move in with him.

The only catch was he and I weren't really lovers, at least not in the normal sense of the word, since we only got together in "that way" every year or two. However, just the fact that he was making up a story about it flattered me and made me think that maybe in another lifetime or in a different situation, it could have happened. My excuse for it never coming true in *this* lifetime was because "I didn't want to ruin the friendship" even though I knew he was in love with me. I knew this was fact because he wrote a song about me to that effect, taped it, and gave it to me as a present. Even so, we were both happy the way it was because we knew nothing would stop us from growing old together. We even promised each other that if we were both single at the age of seventy we would marry each other.

I couldn't believe he had so many stories about me, all of them true. I was glad he was making money at my expense, but I couldn't understand why anybody would be interested in writing about me, much less reading about me. I never thought I was that interesting.

The next story was of a much more serious nature. It was about the time I got sick and had to be hospitalized. I had a boyfriend at the time, but when I suddenly got appendicitis and had to have emergency surgery, my boyfriend was nowhere to be found. So guess who waited along with my mother in the waiting room? It was very traumatic, considering I almost died, and the recovery was difficult. Although I don't recommend surgery as a way to lose weight to anybody, I did lose seventeen pounds.

After I came home, he was the one who nursed me back to health, not my boyfriend. This should have been an indication to me that he was the person I should be with in spite of the "cat problem," but it still didn't register and I married my boyfriend, only to be divorced four years later. This fact was included in the story merely to rub it in that I had made a terrible mistake, even though it happened a long time ago.

So, one story followed another, and before I knew it, there was a collection of ten stories, all about him and me.

In the meantime, he had become a Buddhist, but only took from Buddhism what he found useful and ignored the parts of the religion that didn't make any sense to him. I'd hear him constantly chanting *Nam-myoho-renge-kyo*—especially if anything went wrong. He became a vegetarian, which was remarkable considering he had told me at one point during his meat eating days that he ate meat every day, sometimes with every meal.

I think the stories about the mice and the cats made him rethink his whole philosophy about how animals fit into the whole scheme of the universe. He also started reading the transcendentalists, especially Emerson. Not only did he have books all over the place, he also had Emerson's quotes posted everywhere, including the walls of the bathroom; that way you could sit on the pot and read how you probably shouldn't even have the luxury of having the privilege of using modern plumbing.

The stories kept getting more and more serious, starting with the mouse story and ending with a story about his theory of soul mates. His philosophy of soul mates had to do with what he called the quaternity. At first, I didn't take it seriously, especially when he explained that even though I was included in the quaternity as his point of emotions (the others being mind, spiritual and body) I wasn't his soul mate. Needless to say, I was very disappointed, especially since he had written all these stories where I was the focal point, but I didn't let him know that it upset me. When I saw how important it was to him, I expressed an interest in the theory and began to understand he had a desperate need to know exactly who his soul mate was.

Before, he had been very sarcastic about any kind of religion or anything remotely spiritual, but writing all the stories had made him look at things in a much more spiritual manner and appreciate the life he had. I was glad that I could help him reach that conclusion.

The stories were eventually put into a collection called *K's Stories*. The nearly impossible being obtained, the book became a best seller and the money started pouring in. We were doing book signings, interviews, and were invited to appear on talk shows. I say "we" because, not only did people want to meet the author, they wanted to meet the mysterious and infamous K. I drew the line at the talk show, because I didn't want anybody imposing on my life. I didn't want to have to change my life style because of my newfound notoriety. I was content living in an apartment with my four cats.

He was extremely pleased with how things were going, and he decided to start a second collection of stories. I was very curious about what the inspiration for these stories would be, since he had used every conceivable idea about us in his first collection.

Lately, I'd noticed that he didn't seem to need me in his life as much. He didn't always invite me to do things with him and took someone else, or went by himself to his new friends' parties. I wondered if he had found a replacement for me. He was always telling me if I ever moved away he would have to find a replacement for me on the quaternity. While I hadn't expressed any desire to move away, I had mentioned that at some point I might have to since my job could require it. This concept of "replacement" got me very angry since I couldn't understand how one could replace a person.

I have since found this to be even more difficult to understand with the experience of the death of loved ones, who can never be replaced no matter how hard one tries.

As I thought about the situation more and more, I realized it didn't bother him as much as it bothered me. I even determined that his idea about the cats getting their own place was absurd. How could he have used such a ridiculous idea for a story, and how could people have thought it was so wonderful? What especially angered me was: it was *my* cats that inspired the story at a time when he didn't even like cats.

I vowed I wouldn't call as often, but as I soon discovered, this backfired because he didn't care whether I called or not. And worse, he never returned my calls when I *did* call. Eventually, we weren't talking to each other at all. I was annoyed, but went on with my life as best I could.

To think, it all started with that conversation about angels. I wouldn't be surprised if he used *that* idea for his next book.

When the book did come out, I had to buy it in the bookstore like everybody else. It was a collection of stories called *Angels.* As I thought, the title story was about our discussion, but he didn't acknowledge my input in any way. I had the book for a week before I could muster up the courage to start reading it.

I discovered immediately I did not exist in the new stories, which told about the changes in his life. One had to do with his becoming a vegetarian, another with his obsession with the Transcendentalists, and so on. Just as I had disappeared from his real life, I disappeared from his stories. Also missing was his sense of humor; the new one didn't make me laugh like the last collection.

I tried calling to congratulate him, but some strange woman answered the phone, so I just hung up. Eventually, I did move away and tried to forget about the whole situation even though we had been friends for so long. I started a new life and never heard from him again, and that is how one of the most important relationships in my life ended.

I wish it could have happened exactly as I've related here. The truth of the matter is, what you just read is simply a story, half-truths, what-could-have-beens. Wishful thinking, nothing more.

Although he never wrote the stories within this story, we did either talk about them, or actually live them. He did quit his job: not to become a writer, but because it was too stressful. He already was a writer and had published several things, even writing and producing a one-act play.

Subsequently, he checked himself into a hospital under suicide watch, but his mental condition didn't get any better, only worse. After his sojourn in the hospital, he did become Buddhist and made all those changes in his life. And, in the process, he did lose his sense of humor.

Eventually, we were drawn apart, and, in the end, he took his own life, becoming the angel without wings he had discussed. Yes, he did have great eyelashes. And sadly, we never would marry each other at the age of seventy.

Naturally, I would rather have been estranged from him because of his success, not because of his death. The pain would have been a lot less. This story is just about what could have been and perhaps could still be in a parallel universe, which is where it obviously takes place. At least he would still be alive. I wish there was a way to get there and see him again, but that's another story, which I'll save for another day.

As far as my theory about angels, I still often wonder where the angel was to catch him as he fell.

About the author:

Karin B. Schlenker lives in Hancock, Michigan with her husband and four cats and a dog. She is a German and occasional French Lecturer at Michigan Technological University. Karin has always enjoyed writing, originally starting with poetry when she was twelve. She has only been writing short stories for the past four years and hopes to eventually publish a book of short stories. The story "What Could Have Been" is dedicated to the memory of a dear friend, Barry Ross Walden (11/26/58 -- 01/08/97).

BUT FOR GLORIA
©2006 by Kristen J. Tsetsi

Stanley leans back in his chair so that it rests against the side of the house and props his feet on the rail. He looks at his watch and discovers he's already been outside for an hour, and comfortably. It's getting better. Two weeks ago, he would have come out only to smoke. He doesn't remember exactly when it was he'd first stopped enjoying the porch he'd built, that Christine had helped stain. It was some time after she died, after her sunless Sunday wake, after what he'd believed would never get better, did.

The loss that he and Gloria, their daughter, suffered had weighed on them for more than a year, the house parlor-hushed with drawn curtains because no one thought to open them. Eventually, as they had been told it would, their pain had waned, become bearable, and the life he and Gloria led moved on, uncomplicated, nearly ideal.

Without her mother to talk to, Gloria had slowly begun approaching Stanley. It had started with awkward hugs goodnight that Stanley knew were more for him than for Gloria. But soon, they seemed to be just as much for her. She'd started talking to him while he made dinner. Perched on the counter, hands locked under her thighs, she would watch and ask questions about how long to bake chicken, broil steak, or simmer a sauce. Stanley learned to ask questions once deemed Christine's area by default; questions about homework, friends, and later, boys. But Gloria didn't talk much about the boys.

For a while, Stanley had savored their time together. Until it became too normal. Until it seemed their lives were running too smoothly. Until every smile he and Gloria shared, every dinner they cooked together, every wave she offered to him in the bleachers was a reminder to not take anything for granted. Until every peaceful moment brought with it an unbearable twisting in his chest and stomach, like the butterflies he remembered from the night he first told Christine he loved her. Only, the new feeling wrenched and churned and weighed heavy, not like the light giddiness he associated with Christine.

As more time passed Stanley grew certain he wasn't the only one aware of dangerous normalcy. The whole neighborhood seemed locked in a circle of feigned happiness and suspicious perfection. Colorful stories sprouted from the newspaper's black and white rows, accounts of townsfolk helping one another, raising funds for charities, growing record-sized fruits and vegetables. So he looked to the obituaries, but even the deaths were not out of the ordinary, not unusually tragic. Stanley felt they all existed in a cleaned-up version of a Disney movie in which tragedy was limited to a flat tire or a losing high school basketball team.

He obsessed over the news, watched and waited for something horrific, something reassuring, something happening to someone else. Afternoons, he stood locked behind the window waiting for Gloria to come home from school. When the bus was late, he made frantic phone calls. When Gloria limped, he forgot about soccer and asked who'd hurt her. He worried about pink pork chops and stopped at yellow lights. He panicked when his left arm ached and had driven, more than once, to the hospital before turning around to go home, the pain gone.

When it happened, when the bad feeling—as he called it—came, if he were sitting, he had to stand; if he were standing, he had to walk. Move away from it, leave it behind, outrun it. He got hot without sweating and everything inside him threatened to tear out, to break through his skin. Wherever he was, he had to go somewhere else, somewhere safe, had to talk to someone, anyone, to get his mind off the fear that lingered through the daylight hours and kept him awake at night, easing only after the sun came up. Mornings were calm; a new day, hope in the songs of puddle-bathing sparrows. But by midday it would start again, and at night, when it was at its worst, he smoked, his cigarettes burning to the filter. The smoking helped, because it was something bad in all the good. Something that could get him unless he controlled it.

He used to share porch evenings with Christine. They would put Gloria to bed and go out together, revel in the silent dark, stand with arms around each other, and listen to the leaves of their maple tree brush against one another in the wind. And after, when she was gone and he was alone, he would escape to the porch when the bed felt too large and the house too empty. He went because he sensed her there, felt her standing beside him and smelled her shampoo in the air. But she faded after a time, was pulled from him in a traveling wind, and no matter where he stood, he could no longer smell her.

It was when the dark became a curtain for danger to hide behind, and when rustling trees were footsteps stealing around the side of the house, that smoking stopped being enough. Evenings came early and light breezes squeezed his lungs. Laughter from neighborhood lawns was a cover for the collective fear of the community that, one of these days, something was going to crush them. Stanley knew it would fall on Gloria, or himself, first. The day Stanley knew he had to do it, had to change things, he had stood on the porch enjoying the few minutes of morning calm allowed to him. Blue sky, sparse clouds, dry, crisp air. Gloria was sleeping, not to wake before nine. Practice began at ten, and she liked plenty of rest.

It hit him hard and fast, and earlier than usual. He pulled the chair close and sat. But he couldn't be still, because stillness was death. He got up and walked down the porch steps, out to the sidewalk, and looked for a neighbor to greet. No one. Puddles from the previous night's rain pooled in sidewalk dips and lawn dew glinted. Thick morning haze hung low in the street. Stanley heard the echo of a closing car door, a dull *thud* in the fog. He hurried to the middle of the road and caught a glimpse of Kyle Harrison through a faintly tinted window. Stanley considered running over to him, asking to borrow a lawnmower or hedge clipper, but Stanley's lawn was freshly mowed and he'd never planted hedges.

He went back inside and turned on the TV for noise, for a funny program, for something to take his mind. He sat on the floor, legs pulled to his chest, and concentrated on the woman on TV. Her words—he couldn't make sense of them, couldn't turn them into anything he could use or hold onto. He had to get up, go somewhere. Stanley stumbled to Gloria's bedroom and stood over her a long time, aching to wake her up, to talk to someone, but knew if he did he would only run screaming because nothing could take it away. He couldn't wait for it any more, this thing that was going to happen to her, to himself. It was coming too close; he could feel it.

He had to catch it before it hit, had to protect Gloria.

Before Christine, he'd hunted coyote and, once or twice, fox. He'd stopped to make her happy, but had kept his rifle on a table in the attic behind Christine's old exercise bike. He touched Gloria's hair. If it happened to them it wouldn't happen to him, to Gloria. Burglars and rapists weren't randomly attacked and neither was Dahmer or Bundy, because they did it first. Stanley wasn't like them, but he had to pretend. No one would know he was faking.

Two hours later, he drove her to practice.

"I can get a ride home with Jackie," Gloria said. She flicked the vent back and forth with a finger. *Click, click, click.*

After dropping her off, he drove with sweaty palms down the interstate, punching radio buttons when cars passed and refusing to meet eyes in the rearview mirror. He used to pester Christine about not using her mirrors, and he knew if she were watching him now she would shake a playful finger. But that would be all, because she would understand. She knew him well.

She'd *known* him well.

He parked in the trees. Sat for an hour with the engine running. A schoolbook of Gloria's sat on the floor of the front seat where she'd forgotten it the day before. Stanley tossed it in the back seat, then reached around and shoved it under the front passenger seat. Through the trees and across the interstate, people of varying ages and sexes and sizes went to and from their cars in the mall parking lot. Stanley got out of his car and grabbed his rifle from the trunk and brought it with him to the front seat, rested it on the vinyl cushion just inside of the open window. He'd parked deep in the woods, had driven along a path with tire-grooves so long since used that they were nearly hidden under new growth. Any nearby houses were abandoned, their windows broken out, paint all but gone, the frames leaning dangerously to one side or the other.

He peered through the scope, focused not on the target but the center of the crosshairs. He would just sit there, nothing more. Just point and that would do it.

His finger went naturally to the trigger and the scope rested snugly on his cheekbone. His hands were sweaty, so he rubbed one then the other on his pants and took aim again.

Blurs of red then orange then white passed back and forth in the crosshairs, urban targets in animal range, slow, careless, fearless, and ignorant. Coming, going, gone. Here, there, close, far, but never too close or too far; the range was perfect one way or the other. He closed his eyes to their faces, blinked fast and aimed down. If, even just this once, if he could just do it, maybe this once would handle everything, and he'd never have to do it again. Something trickled down his face and he rubbed it away from his mouth, and white came into view and it glowed bright like the sun through an unprotected periscope. If he shot now, that periscope would never reflect on his house, on Gloria's late-night light, on the cherry of his cigarette glowing bright on his dark porch. Shoot and it won't happen to you, shoot now and it will never come back, shoot now, now, now.

He didn't stay put to see it fall. That was how he had to look at things, the first time. He didn't know what he'd hit, only that it had started out white. As soon as the shot was fired, he was out of the car and tossing the rifle in the trunk and getting back in the driver's seat and heading home. He knew he'd hit—there was no way he could have missed. And it was on the way home, on the stretch between city and suburb, that he breathed, that he discovered it hadn't been sweat streaming down his face but tears, that the fire in his stomach had cooled and settled, that the thought of spending time with Gloria filled him with unrestricted joy, that the rush of air through the window didn't make him wonder if it would not be long before he'd never feel the wind again.

Stanley remembers that day with mixed feelings, and he doesn't imagine they'll ever unmix, much as he might like to feel only guilt. Because he knows he should. He feels guilty about not feeling guilty. He isn't sure which is worse.

The front door swings open. Stanley turns to see his daughter with one hand on the doorknob, the other barely managing to hang onto a sandwich, her nightly snack.

"It happened again," she says.

Stanley follows her inside.

The woman in the parking lot dropped before reaching her car, they say on the news. Stanley remembers. How her back had pushed forward, as if someone had shoved her from behind. From Stanley's position behind the trees, he'd watched her purchases spill out of the bag. Some kind of over the counter medicine, a candle, a box of film. He sees all kinds of things through the scope, things others can't.

Gloria lies on the floor, legs crossed at the ankles, head resting on a cushion she's pulled from the chair. She'd done this for as long as Stanley can remember. He and Christine gave up trying to get her to sit on furniture fairly early on.

Gloria, brushing hair away from her forehead, listens to the news. She's inherited her nervous habit from Christine. When she used to worry about her parents, or Gloria, or something at work,

Christine's long fingers would rake her hair, temple to neck.

"You okay, kiddo?" Stanley pokes the pillows with a foot.

"I don't even want to leave the house," she says, her sandwich sitting uneaten atop a folded paper towel on the floor. Gloria, seventeen, had never used a night light until after the third shooting. She leaves her bedroom door open now and looks out the window before going from house to car on schooldays. Stanley won't tell her that a nightlight doesn't matter, that these things happened during the day. Since the shootings had started, he'd made her come home right after school. Everyone knows it isn't safe to be outside. The neighbors will think funny of him if he doesn't keep her home.

Gloria stands and puts the cushion back on the chair. "I can't watch anymore."

"I don't want you to be scared," he says.

"I can't help it." She stands in front of him and stuffs her hands in her pockets. "Do you think they'll catch him?"

He thinks about it, wonders if he's been careful enough. "I don't think so." He changes the channel when commercials come.

"When will things get back to normal?"

"I don't know. Soon, I hope."

Gloria gives him a goodnight kiss on the cheek. He watches her walk down the hall to her room. She used to walk like a boy, clunky and stiff. Now there's more fluidity, a womanly swing in her arms that matches the sway of her hips. Christine would have loved to see this, to know her daughter past age fifteen. When Gloria was a baby, Christine could sit with her for hours and talk secret mother-daughter talk about what it meant to be a girl, what it would mean to be a woman. Stanley listened sometimes, outside the door, wanting to know their secrets. Christine had said, before Gloria was born, that she didn't care what sex they ended up with, but when Gloria finally came out, head red and silent, eyes tight shut, and the doctor announced it was a girl, Christine had closed her own eyes, taken a long, slow breath and, smiling, had asked to hold her.

Stanley's bond with Gloria isn't as strong as Christine's used to be, but he enjoys working on it. If not for Gloria, he doesn't know what he would have done after Christine's death.

He's doing the right thing.

He watches the news long after Gloria goes to bed. Topics shift from the shootings to market reports to a possible war in Iraq, but they always circle back. Prerecorded TV journalists stand under umbrellas in the rain where the latest shooting has taken place, this one in the parking lot of a drug store. Reporters on one channel speculate about a shell casing found in the trees where he had stood, while on another channel different reporters discuss sketches of a tan Buick that had been seen at more than one crime scene, a possible clue. Stanley doesn't own a tan Buick. The hours he works at the auto-parts store are short and sporadic, the life insurance money is dwindling to nothing. He still drives the old VW bug he and Christine bought when they first married.

He wants to drink when he sits down at night to watch the news, but he'd never responded well to any kind of drug. He'd experimented in college, as that seemed to be the rule. Alcohol had made him sick in a friend's sink. He'd tried cocaine and had fainted, fallen out of his chair. At a party a week later, he'd tried again with the same results. Months later someone had offered him marijuana. Stanley had been assured it was mild and would make him "mellow." He'd taken two, maybe three hits, and had come to on the floor with his head between two vertical blind flaps. Christine was there. She had been the one to tug his arm and tell him it was time to get up.

He wants to not have to watch the news at all. But being confronted while lucid is a punishment he has to endure. He has to see the eyes of those brave enough to answer reporters' questions, when they have no idea whether or not the shooter is still there, hiding, waiting. He doesn't have what they have. If he were one of them, one of the unknowing, random, he would never leave his house. Not for anything. And he almost was one of them, before he fixed everything.

A woman, a possible witness the reporter holding the microphone says, looks through the TV at Stanley. Her dark hair is pulled back in a loose ponytail and her face is young, kind. Early wrinkles have set in around eyes that are green, not bright, but deep. *You are hated*, they say.

Stanley fumbles with the power button on the remote and turns the screen black. He steps back out onto the porch and stands in the dark. Stars fall quiet on the houses across the street, their light not carried away by the heavy wind, and the moon shines gray on yellow leaves of the tree in his yard. Bluish glows light up his neighbors' living rooms and groaning porch swings hang empty. Two weeks ago, he could have called across to any of his neighbors and received a return greeting over the smoke of charcoal grills.

Stanley feels for the single cigarette he keeps in his breast pocket. He used to smoke a pack a day, but had cut down after Christine died. Someone had to be there for Gloria. He puts the cigarette between his lips, but they don't tighten around it fast enough and it falls. He bends to pick it up and a loose board creaks under his foot. He presses it again, testing it. He won't fix it. The creak comforts him, leaves him sure the rest of the porch is sound. To fix it would be to invite a larger flaw somewhere else, later, when he isn't expecting it. Perfection can't exist without flaws.

He lights the cigarette and the smoke scratches down his throat and comes out in a short stream, whipped instantly away. Gloria used to watch when he smoked in the car and would tell him how unhealthy it was that after three clean breaths smoke still came out of his nose. She is proud of him now for smoking just seven a week. He tells her it's for her.

Stanley read a story in the paper once about a man who didn't smoke or use chewing tobacco but who had somehow developed tongue cancer. They'd cut off a third of his tongue and the radiation treatments made him vomit. Stanley had never known anyone with cancer, but had seen television shows about cancer survivors. Treatments could last a day, depending on the type, and nausea could last up to two days. A woman being interviewed wore a scarf tied around her head and the skin under her eyes bled into her cheeks. The hand she used to scratch her nose was attached to an arm so thin it could break easily as a stick.

Stanley could have quit smoking if he'd wanted to. Cutting down to one a day hadn't been as difficult as people said. But bad things happened to people who were too careful.

Stanley flicks the cigarette onto the lawn and pulls the chair under him. Autumn had always been his favorite season. And Christine's. She'd once compared the way light from streetlamps caught scattered leaves on the road to sunshine on quartz specks. He'd never forgotten that because he'd never have thought of it himself. She thought of things like that. They used to take late night walks, Stanley on the swept sidewalk, Christine in the gutter where leaves collected. Each of her steps would be a kick into a dry, weightless clump, and she would lift it with her foot and fan a spray of brown and yellow and orange in front of her, like a steam liner slicing rainbow waves.

Stanley puts his feet up on the railing. Gloria's bedside lamp, which she often forgets to turn off, casts a rectangular beam on the porch and the trunk of their maple tree. He can take the dark, now. It's as if the sinking sun carries sound away with it, like matter sucked into a black hole, and leaves everything else in expert detail. Paint chips on siding are airbrushed; plants are sparse brushstrokes on black stems and stalks lost somewhere behind.

He can't go back to the news, yet. This reclaimed serenity cannot go unappreciated. If he doesn't savor the dark, the night sounds, the calm, people will have died for nothing. If nothing else, they deserve this.

About the author:

Kristen Tsetsi holds an MFA from Minnesota State University Moorhead, where several of her short stories have been published in the school's literary journal, *Red Weather Magazine*. Two additional short stories, "The Nature of Things" and "In the

Wheatfield," have been published in online journals *Against the Grain* and *Expository Magazine* (respectively). She pushes herself to experiment with several genres and has experienced moderate success with both stage and screen plays. Two of her one-act plays, "The Girl on the Swing" and "Gun in the Corner," saw production, and her story-to-screen adaptation of her short story "The Fittest" was screened at the annual Fargo Film Festival. "Like Cockatoos," an original full-length screenplay, earned her the Robert Carothers Distinguished Writers Award. Kristen currently lives in Rochester, NY with her husband, three cats, and two ecosphere shrimp, and is working on her first novel.

DOWN FROM THE MOUNTAIN
©2006 by Phillip Lynne

Rain drifted off the dark lake in sheets, driven by a cool wind that swept through the trees at the water's edge and up the hill to where Oscar Canaday sat on his screened-in front porch. He was silent, staring across the lake, his face set in stone.

There was movement behind him. "Are you coming to bed? It's after two."

"In a minute, Kate."

She came to stand behind his rocking chair. "You haven't slept in three days."

"My brain won't let me. And our bed's not the same. *Nothing's* the same anymore."

Her hand was cool on his cheek. "I know. I feel like I'm on another planet. But it will get better with time. I've done a lot of praying these last few days, looking for answers."

"Did you get any?"

"Only, what's done is done. God's will has been served and we must accept it."

Anger swelled inside him. "God's will, Kate? Is *that* God's will?" He pointed across to the enclosed end of the porch.

A brilliant flash of lightning tore the night open, revealing a flag-draped casket supported on both ends by funeral sawhorses.

"Everything is God's will, Oscar. He's in control. It's not up to us to question Him."

Oscar got to his feet. "Don't you understand? I *have* to question it. I *have* to know why my son died in a war thousands of miles away. I *have* to ask why he was ripped from this world before he had a chance to live."

"You must have faith, Oscar."

"Faith? I *had* faith. I had faith that my only son would outlive me, that he would grow up and have kids of his own, and that he would bury *me* on the mountain." He moved to the casket and spread his hands on it. "I should be in there, not Shawn."

Kate Canaday crossed the porch and put her arms around him from behind. "Don't say that."

"But, what am I supposed to do, Kate? How can I go on? I can't handle this."

"You've always been the toughest man in town, Oscar. Nothing fazes you. All those years at the steel mill, you never let the work or the hours get to you. Not so much as a whimper as you turned around and went back for more. Being tough is your life. But, this is not the time for tough. Now is the time for tenderness. Let it go, Oscar. Let everything go. Cry for our son."

Oscar turned toward her, his eyes wide in the darkness. "I can't. Not until I understand. Not until I...."

She hugged him as the moon emerged from the clouds and laid a silver road of light across the lake.

Next morning, the funeral was held at the Canaday home, the front yard covered with white folding chairs. With few exceptions, the entire population of town was there, cars lining the dirt road. Baskets of flowers ringed the gathering, sweetening the air with their perfume and steam rose from the lake as the sun warmed the water. Pine trees and blue skies formed a ceiling that no cathedral could ever rival.

Reverend Rosenthal took his place behind an oak podium and thanked God for the life of Shawn and the blessings each of them had received from knowing such a kind, thoughtful young man. He asked that Shawn's body be committed to the earth, and that his soul be allowed to wander on streets of gold.

Throughout the ceremony, Oscar stared at the casket, the words of the minister nothing more than background noise, drowned by his own thoughts, the questions, the wondering, the doubts.

"Oscar?" Kate's voice was a million miles away.

He tore his eyes away from the casket. "What?"

"It's time to go up the mountain, honey."

He stood, pulled at the uncomfortable wool suit that Kate had insisted he wear, then put on a beat-up, brown fedora. The hat didn't match the suit but he didn't feel normal without it. "Let's be getting on with it, then."

The pallbearers placed the casket on an old carriage built by Shawn's grandfather. Oscar himself took the reins and walked beside the carriage, guiding the two work horses on a path that wound its way up the side of Canaday Mountain. Kate was five steps behind him, the townspeople following at a respectful distance.

Above the tree line, Reginald McIngle stood beside the grave he had been digging since before sunup. He removed his hat and held it over his heart as the carriage approached. He then stepped forward and clasped Oscar's hand before taking the reins from him.

"I loved Shawn like he was my own," McIngle said. "I can't tell you how sorry I am about all this, Oscar."

Oscar said, "Thank you, Reggie. I appreciate your hard work today," and stepped aside as the pallbearers lifted the casket again.

Reverend Rosenthal opened his Bible and asked everyone to pray with him. Again, Oscar was lost in his thoughts, his eyes riveted on the casket. As the casket softly thumped at the bottom of the grave, he looked up. People were beginning to wander back down the mountain in small groups, and he watched Kate as she said her silent farewells, dropping nineteen roses, one at a time, onto the casket.

"One for each of his years," she explained. Looking at him sharply, she added, "Are you all right?"

"Yeah, sure. I'm fine."

McIngle was clutching his hat in both hands. "Oscar, I should fill it in now."

Silently, Oscar removed his jacket and tossed it away, the tie following quickly. He grabbed the shovel and buried the blade in the pile of dirt.

McIngle cleared his throat. "Here, Oscar, that's my job."

Kate reached out and took her husband's arm. "Come down to the house."

Shaking her off, he said, "I have to do this, Kate. Leave me alone."

She looked deep into his eyes, saw something there, and then nodded. "We'll be there when you're finished." She took Reggie McIngle by the arm and they walked off.

As silence returned to the mountain, Oscar worked steadily, perspiration beading on his forehead, sweat stains spreading across his shirt. The casket boomed hollowly as each shovelful of dirt was tossed in. He absorbed the sound, using its rhythm to pace himself, to steady his labored breath. He absorbed, too, the pain that began to burn across his back and arm muscles. He welcomed the pain as a way to transfer his frustrations through the shovel, plunging its blade into the dirt again and again.

Two hours later, his breath all but torn from his body, he realized the grave was full. He leaned on the shovel and mopped the sweat from his eyes. Staring at the fresh earth, he was overtaken by emotions that clutched at his throat and compressed his heart.

With an angry shout, he spun on his heel, slinging the shovel in a wide arc before releasing it to tumble slowly into the air, down the mountainside, and through the branches of a cedar tree.

"*There!*" Oscar shouted, turning his face to the sky. "There's my son! You wanted him bad enough to cut his life short, take him!" He took a step forward, lost his footing on the loose dirt, and fell to his knees. "But, I had him first!" He tried to stand, but his legs were rubber. "I had him first, goddamit! And I wasn't finished with him. There were so many things we didn't do. So many things we should have done. We weren't finished yet; can't you see that?"

"Just who the devil you yelling at, Pop?"

Startled, Oscar looked around. Shawn Canaday sat on a nearby boulder, leaning back on his hands, one knee raised. He wore a baggy pair of pants and a flannel shirt, a hat identical to Oscar's perched on his head at a jaunty angle.

Oscar grinned and replied, "At whoever's listening. What are you doing here?"

"Heard you yelling and came to see what all the fuss is about. You sounded right mad."

"I was. *Am*."

"What about?"

Oscar frowned, trying to focus his thoughts. "Because you're dead." He looked up suddenly. "My dear Lord, Shawn, you're *dead*."

"Really? Then shouldn't *I* be the one raising a ruckus?"

Oscar rubbed his forehead. "I don't understand this. How are you here?"

Shawn shrugged. "Beats me." He squinted at his father. "You don't seem real torn up about me being gone."

"Huh?"

"I mean, aren't people supposed to cry and carry on at funerals? You look like you haven't dropped a tear. Why ain't you crying, Pop?"

Oscar found it impossible to meet his son's eyes. "I don't know. I've tried, Shawn, but I can't."

"Still the tough hombre, eh? Remember when I stepped on that rusty nail behind the barn? Went straight through my boot. It took a bit, but I got to the house with the board still attached to my foot."

Oscar nodded. "I remember you hopping around on one foot like an idiot and pointing at the board."

Shawn's laugh filled the mountaintop. "Mom about passed out when you yanked the board off and dumped me in the rain barrel so I didn't get blood all over everything."

Oscar was chuckling now. "You soaked your foot in that barrel until your skin was gray and wrinkled. My Lord, but you were strong. And didn't cry a bit."

Shawn's smile faded. "Not on the *outside*, Pop. My guts were in a knot, and I wanted to cry, I *needed* to cry, but I couldn't."

"Why not?"

"You were there."

"Huh?"

"I couldn't cry in front of you, Pop. You always told me that only sissies cry."

"My Lord, Shawn, you were only five years old with a nail the size of Texas through your foot! I wouldn't have thought you were a sissy."

"I couldn't take the risk. I had to make you proud of me. That was more important than crying."

Oscar bit his lower lip. "If you had, I'd have bawled right along with you."

"Really? Well, weren't we a couple of hardheaded tough guys, eh? Sitting around and waiting for the other guy to start crying."

Oscar nodded. "I guess we were pretty silly. But I was the father and fathers aren't supposed to cry."

"So that's what's stopping you? You can't cry because you're the father?"

"I...I guess so."

"Well, wake up and smell the bacon, Pop!" Shawn said, opening his arms. "You ain't a father no more. I'm dead, remember? And last time I checked, I was the only child."

Something almost electrical passed through Oscar's body, grabbing at his heart. "What do you mean, not a father? I'll always be a father. *Your* father."

"Got to have a kid to be a father and, in case you haven't noticed, you ain't got one no more."

Oscar gasped and felt a rock-hard lump congeal in his throat, threatening to steal his breath away yet again. "I will *always* be a father."

"Of who, Pop? No, wait; guess I can't call you 'Pop' anymore, huh?"

Oscar's eyes burned and seemed to swell out of their sockets. "I will always…" he managed to say before his strength drained and he fell to his knees. A tear, warm and moist, trailed down his cheek and he lifted a finger to it. He stared at the drop for a moment as if studying it.

"Shawn…" he began. A sudden thrill passed through his body, shaking his very bones and causing him to sit down hard in the dirt. His vision clouded as he looked up at his son through tear-filled eyes.

The boy left the rock, coming to kneel next to his father. "It's okay, Pop. I know you're my father. I just had to get the waterworks going. Let it go now. Let *me* go now."

Oscar Canaday surrendered himself, giving in to emotions so long repressed. Grief flowed to the surface, venting itself in tears and sobs as he learned how to cry again.

Kate, sitting on the front porch, heard movement on the trail and turned from her conversation with Reverend Rosenthal. Her husband was approaching the house with his usual purposeful stride, but there was something different. Something in his eyes. Something in his face. Something that brought a smile to her heart.

Reverend Rosenthal got to his feet and met him in the yard. "You've finally come down from the mountain, Oscar."

"I have, Reverend. More than you'll ever know."

About the author:

Phillip Lynne lives in Knoxville, TN, where he continues to bang out stories as they pop into his head.

OPERATION MICKEY MOUSE
©2006 by Catherine Lev

The headquarters received intelligence to the effect that grenade-launchers, AK-47s, and explosives were being stored in Al-Shaheed Mosque. The mosque was in a poor Shiite neighborhood, where one could rarely see an unveiled woman, but could see plenty of portraits of Imam Ali, the successor of Prophet Mohammed. On every portrait the eighth-century Imam was armed with a modern-day rifle, but that did not seem to bother anyone. Americans usually did not venture into that neighborhood unless they had an operation to conduct, and even on the hottest day they would not stop to buy watermelons from a roadside stand.

On that day, however, they *were* involved in an operation. Captain Ingram's company was tasked with surrounding the Al-Shaheed Mosque and conducting the search. The soldiers circled the mosque without incident and waited over two hours for the Imam to finish his sermon.

The mosque occupied a small plot of land enclosed by an opaque clay wall. The wall was adorned with banners—white elaborate lettering on black material—and the same ubiquitous portraits. Nothing inside the mosque could be seen from the street except the top portion of a battered prayer tower. Judging by the fact that the Imam's sermon was being transmitted over a loudspeaker, not all the faithful fitted in the actual mosque building and some of them listened in the courtyard.

Captain Ingram parked his Humvee across from the mosque and now sat on the passenger seat, his legs dangling from the truck, his rifle across his lap. There was a soldier behind the wheel and an Iraqi interpreter on the back seat. Without taking his eyes off the mosque, Captain Ingram distractedly peeled an orange and thoughts of the operation haunted his mind.

Before the operation began, Colonel Robinette summoned Ingram to his office. For no less than half an hour, Colonel Robinette lectured him on the necessity to be extremely careful: "Offending the religious sensibilities of local nationals...uncalled for public relations nightmare...."

Captain Ingram nodded in agreement, interjecting a few *Yes, sirs* and *I understand, sirs* here and there. However, both he and Colonel Robinette knew that no one could project how the residents of the Al-Shaheed neighborhood would respond to any given situation.

Captain Ingram could never quite understand the people he was sent to liberate. They answered rough handling with servility, but acts of kindness generated insults and complaining. They had put up with Saddam for so many years, but were not above killing someone for smoking a cigarette during the fast for Ramadan. They beat one such poor Joe within an inch of his life and dragged him to the American checkpoint. If the checkpoint hadn't been close to the mosque, the unfortunate man would have bled to death.

The orange had long been eaten, but the sermon dragged on and on. Captain Ingram turned to the interpreter. "Kammal, what is he saying?"

"Are you sure you want to know?"

"I am sure. I want to know what is on their minds."

Kammal listened. "He says the Americans attacked Iraq because the Zionists, ruling the world, told them to."

"Wow, I didn't know that Jews ruled the world" snickered the driver "Not that it benefits me any..."

"Cut the sarcasm, Private Silverman," said Captain Ingram

"What else is he saying?"

Kammal listened again. "He says that all Americans engage in orgies."

"I wish..." began Silverman, but decided not to test the commander's patience.

For a few minutes, all three listened to the ravings coming from the loudspeaker.

"He says that all American soldiers are sex maniacs and they wear special glasses to look through the veils of Islamic women."

"I didn't know there was anything to look at!" Silverman would just not quit.

"What glasses?" Captain Ingram asked.

"Night-vision goggles."

They listened some more.

"He says...how should I put it?" Kammal stammered.

"Put it like it is."

"He says the Americans love unclean animals and that every American family owns a Mickey Mouse."

Ingram and Silverman stared at the interpreter in stunned disbelief.

"Are you sure?" Ingram finally asked.

"What are you staring at me for?" Kammal protested indignantly. "You think I am responsible for this fool? Besides, I am a Christian."

"So, every American family has a pet called Mickey Mouse." Silverman verified, giggling under his breath.

"Yes. He says it is a ravenous mouse, the size of a jackal, and with big ears."

At this point not even Captain Ingram could conceal a smile. As for Private Silverman, he was bent over laughing.

Suddenly, Kammal perked up his ears. "That's it. The service is over. They are about to come out."

Captain Ingram got back into serious mode, jumped off the Humvee, and signaled to a squad of soldiers waiting in the nearby bushes. Meanwhile, the gate in the clay wall opened, and no less than three dozen men burst out at once, carrying a white-bearded, black-turbaned Imam on their shoulders. Ingram knew that the black turban signified someone descended from Prophet Mohammed. The captain winced inside.

The gate continued to disgorge the parishioners and soon the whole mosque was surrounded with a screaming, chanting crowd.

Accompanied by Kammal and a squad of soldiers, Captain Ingram stepped towards the Imam. "Tell him, that 1 have an order from the Coalition Provisional Authority to search this mosque for contraband weapons. We promise not to damage the building and not to handle objects of religious value."

Kammal repeated the words in Arabic. The Imam responded, the expression on his face requiring no translation.

"He says he is not going to allow unclean dogs into the mosque."

"Does he mean the police dogs?"

"No, he means you and your soldiers."

Captain Ingram looked back at his "unclean dogs," communicating silently with them with his eyes. He glanced at Private Silverman, who was crouched by the vehicle with all traces of levity gone from his face.

Captain Ingram thought for a second, then turned to Kammal and said, "Tell him that if we do not search the mosque today, 1 will have a hundred Mickey-Mouses airlifted here from Kuwait. They will devour all the dry goods in this neighborhood and eat at the foundation of the mosque."

After hearing the translation, the Imam recoiled. He studied the occupiers' faces. Something about their expressions tipped him that this time it would be better not to kick up a fuss. He stepped aside in silence.

Meanwhile, the other soldiers restrained the crowd. Standing in the frame of the gate, Captain Ingram looked back at the interpreter, the search team, and the soldiers providing security. His face was as serious and focused as usual. Only those who knew him well could detect an unusual mischievous twinkle in his eyes.

"Let's go, gentlemen," said Captain Ingram. "We've got Mickey on our side"

About the author:

Catherine Lev was born in Russia and came to America at age 13. She went to college and law school in New York City and served as JAG attorney in Germany, Texas and Iraq.

TAKE THIS JOB AND LOVE IT
©2006 by Ryan Bennett

It's hard for a lot of people to remember, but a person's first job can be an exhilarating experience. With the exception of being an Indonesian refugee forced into child labor in a sweat shop, the first day at work can be one of the most uplifting and memorable days of one's life. There is such a feeling of pride as you take this first of many important steps into adulthood. You can always sense your friends' jealousy when they ask you if you want to hang out at the mall or something, and you get to reply: "No can do. I've got to go *work* at the mall." Then two weeks later, when you finish your shift and you bump into your friend who is drooling over a new ninja video game in a store window, you can *buy* the ninja video game with your sweet new paycheck and beat it before you even let him play it once.

It's a pretty sweet deal: living at home and being able to blow every last dollar of your hard work on music, movies, sodas, diners, and one-hundred-and-fifty-dollar basketball shoes that serve no other purpose than to help you throw air balls every time you get a half-assed basketball game together with two of your friends maybe once a year.

That first two weeks of work go by pretty fast with the sweet dreams of money in your pocket vastly approaching. I've always imagined everyone's optimistic view as they finished their first day of work as an employed citizen, to be one of confidence, aspirations, and achievement. Hopefully it doesn't end on a sour note of shame, degradation, loss, hopelessness, and failure.

After spending another evening chugging multiple cans of Mountain Dew, I gathered up all of the cans I could to get that amazing Michigan ten-cent refund. Sadly, consuming an entire twenty-four pack only gives you two dollars and forty cents, which wasn't even close to what I needed to see a movie with my friends. My mom informed me that I couldn't mow the lawn any more than three times a week and I had reached my quota yesterday and spent the five bucks on a twenty-four pack of Mountain Dew.

So, instead of seeing a movie with my friends I made time excruciatingly crawl by for my morn by being jacked up on caffeine, making prank calls, and screaming at the top of my lungs. At the peak of her frustration, she declared that the answer to all of my—and mostly her—problems was for me to get a job. She threw me in the car and hauled me around town to fill out dishwasher applications at nearly every restaurant lining our suburban strip mall landscape.

After a couple of fruitless places, I hesitantly walked into the somewhat new and absurdly named Rio Grand Steakhouse. A middle-aged, big-boned, jolly fellow named Mike gave me an application and told me he'd like to talk in detail after I filled it out.

A rush of confidence filled my spirit. Wow! I must have really made quite an impression when I asked for an application to wash dishes. People were starting to take notice of this young man looking for the corporate ladder. Through the sheer monotony of filling out the application, it actually crossed my mind to buy a suit. Yes, sir, I was on the road to respect. Perhaps when I get home I should research some various stocks and my options for them. I was most definitely going to have to talk morn into getting a fax machine. Oh, and an espresso machine. I would surely have to locate a reliable dry cleaner shop, and a recipe for a delicious power lunch.

After fifteen minutes, I had finished the application and Mike had returned holding a red and a yellow shirt. He sat down in the booth with me and held the application in front of his face. It seriously looked like his eyes crossed for the two seconds he pretended to look at it.

The strong scent of ale blew over me as he began talking. "Apple cation looks good. What are you in, hikes school?"

"Yes sir. I'm in marching band," I said, somehow believing this skill added to my resume.

"Whatime yotta school?" he stammered.

"Around three," I replied.

"So, you can be here round four ery day?" he said as his eyes seemed to suddenly widen and say *Don't screw me on this answer, kid.*

"Absolutely, sir, no problem," I eagerly stated.

"Alright, Brian, you got the job. Can you start this weekend?" he asked.

I nodded and was handed my two Rio Grand Steakhouse staff tee shirts. Our meeting was adjourned after a handshake, and I walked back through the restaurant as one of the waitresses caught my eye. She smiled and asked how the interview went and I held up my two new shirts in proud response. Before I walked out into the parking lot, I hid the shirts in the back of my pants to appear at a loss once again to my mom as I got back into the car.

"You were in there for a while," she said. "Did you get to talk to a manager this time?"

"Yep," I said, trying to hold back the surprise.

"Well, what happened?" she asked absently.

"Oh, the same old same old...and that I'll BE WORKING AS A DISHWASHER THIS WEEKEND AT THE RIO GRAND STEAKHOUSE!!!"

I guess I was kind of expecting her to react like one of my teenage friends and scream and honk the horn or something, instead of the simple smile and plain "congratulations" that I received. Looking back, I'm not sure if *I* could really go buck wild for someone who has just been hired to spend their free time repetitively scraping off half eaten mashed potatoes with cigarettes stubbed out in them, either. So I think the plain fact that I was going to be out of her hair a lot more was the main reason that brought a smile to her face.

The whole thing definitely wasn't an infectious celebration. When I told my friends, one of them told me their older brother was a dishwasher once, and he had a hard time meeting girls because he constantly smelled like rotten fish. It didn't help much to try to stick up for myself by explaining that I would be working at a steak house, and would come home smelling like meat. It was also a bummer to learn that a bunch of my friends were going that weekend to my friend's parent's cabin to water ski and ride four-wheelers.

"Yeah, well, maybe in a couple of weeks, I'll buy my *own* four-wheeler," I desperately said as they walked away.

The next couple of days leading up to that weekend found me thumbing through catalogs and looking at four-wheeler prices. Or, hanging out with friends at a diner and secretly studying the busboys and dishwashers as they came out to clear off tables. I would mentally take note of what table they should have hit first, and to wipe the crumbs off the booth seats, and maybe even go that extra mile to help the servers by filling up condiments or changing ashtrays.

Though I noticed it in all of the dishwashers, I assured myself I wasn't going to be as pissed, greasy, and lonely as the ones I had been watching. Not me. I had ambition. I had dreams of buying a four-wheeler in my suburban neighborhood with absolutely no place to ride it and no purpose for owning it other than to prove to my friends that it was pretty cool to have a job as a dishwasher.

Oh, yes. The ladies would surely look past my meat aroma when I pulled into school on a god-damned four-wheeler in the middle of winter. Hey, maybe I wouldn't even have to go to school anymore! I was about to become a working citizen. Yeah, I was only a dishwasher, but every successful entrepreneur started from the bottom and then slowly built their empire.

If I dropped out of school now and dedicated all of my time to this job, by the time my friends graduate I could be a manager at the Rio Grand Steakhouse. My friends could come to *my* cabin and use *my* four-wheelers. How much did managers make? It is a steakhouse, and steaks are pretty much the most expensive dinners there are, so it's got to be a ton of dough. Probably the same amount as a doctor or lawyer, and law and medical school takes something like six years. I bet I could be financially on par with them by two.

Sorry, Bill Gates, looks like you won't be on the cover of Forbes forever. There's a new dishwasher in town four-wheeling his way to financial domination!

I came home from school before my first day of work to find my grandparents over for a visit and to congratulate me on this step into adulthood. My grandmother gave me a hug and a kiss and told me that all of the girls would come chasing me. That was pretty uplifting to hear, since I seemed to develop four or five massive blackhead zits every couple of hours from a daily dose of pizza, soda, and video games.

My grandfather was a lot more serious and had obviously planned out on their two-hour drive what to say to me. He had made a lot of money being a salesman in the automobile industry in Detroit and had a couple of plaques that were also clocks which praised his decades of work. He solemnly gave me a speech that involved some key words like *dedication, commitment,* and *success.* I also noticed the change in tone go down towards the end of the speech and words like *sacrifice, draining,* and *dreams.*

Ultimately though, everyone in my family was proud and glad they were with me before my first day of work. I want to say my mom made me a cake or something, but I seriously only remember that it was raining outside. The rest is a complete blur, like when a quarterback is sacked so hard he goes into a coma. Regaining consciousness a couple of months later, he doesn't exactly remember who he was going to pass to or where they were on the field. His memories consist only of what team they were playing, and then the paralyzing hit.

My mom drove me to work and dropped me off. The early dinner crowd started arriving in their pick-up trucks. They were generally hefty white men in their fifties, wearing dress shirts tucked into jeans and cowboy hats above their plump, red faces. I took a deep breath and strolled in wearing my bright red Rio Grand Steakhouse shirt.

A different, more slender and sober manager approached me, with a disturbing look of confusion. "Can I help you?" he asked while oblivious to my tee shirt.

"Hi, my name is Ryan," I said without receiving a reaction. "Uh, Mike hired me as a dishwasher. "

"Oh, oh, oh, oh, all right. Yeah, I think he mentioned that to me," he anxiously replied.

He introduced himself with a generic name and introduced me quickly to a couple of the waitresses. After a few polite smiles, I was then escorted to the dish room. The harsh odor that immediately hit me was a nauseating mix of meat, ketchup, copper, and—surprisingly—fish. I was given a thirty second explanation on how to rinse plates that obviously had been sitting there for hours, set them on a rack, put it into the machine, and close the door. Repeat. There was a separate rack for silverware.

"Think you can handle it?" he asked without sarcasm.

"I hope so," I replied, already feeling dizzy from the scent of spoiled milk.

With that, he was gone and I felt horribly alone. The walls were comprised of blank, scummy tiles, and there was a constant buzzing sound coming from somewhere within the room. I looked at the bus tub in front of me that contained a hideous mix of cups and plates in a pool of plastic creamer containers, meat blood, fat chunks, fish bones, and was that...? Yep, Corn Flakes. How in the hell?

Suddenly, a waiter slammed through the door with an overflowing bus tub and dropped it on the table in front of me. "Hey, newbie," he said as a smirk formed over his braces, "better get a move on."

He vanished as quickly as he had appeared. I looked around a second for some gloves and found none. I took a deep breath and picked up the first dish in one hand and the spray nozzle with the other. I held the dish so it faced me, and squeezed the spray nozzle trigger. A hot blast of ketchup and water bounced right back into my face and eyes. I let out a little scream, dropped the plate, and it shattered. I panicked and looked at the door to make sure no one saw me break a dish in the first minute of working there. I bent down and the ketchup on my face started to sting my eyes as I nervously picked up the broken plate pieces. I quickly threw them in the garbage and started moving fast to clean the other dishes and load them on the rack. When it was loaded, I slid the rack into the machine and closed the door.

A smile came to my lips and, with my sleeve, I wiped the rest of the ketchup water off my face. The machine stopped making noise and I opened the door and pulled the rack of dishes back out. More than half of them still had crusty food caked onto them. The door suddenly opened again and scared the hell out of me, as the manager stood in the doorway.

"Hey, Ryan, you got a second?" he asked politely, "I guess Mike never entered you into the computer, so I've got to get some information from you. You want to get paid, don't you?"

I nodded and wondered if that meant I wasn't going to get paid for the one rack of dishes I'd halfway cleaned already. I followed him to his office, which had tons of papers laying around in it, bits of mashed potatoes on the ground, and a very old computer on the middle of a desk. I took a seat next to him and we stared at the computer screen together. He asked me for my full name, my address, my social security number, and then my date of birth, which he didn't type in as fast as the other information.

"Nineteen seventy-seven? That would mean that you are..." he asked while squinting.

"Fifteen," I replied.

"Oh, geez," he said while exhaling loudly, "I don't know if Mike told you this, and I don't know what he was thinking, but you have to be at least sixteen to work here."

A lump formed in my throat. My butt cheeks clenched. My voice cracked when I tried to speak again. For a good ten seconds or so I sounded like a stuttering version of Bobcat Goldthwait. I finally got out that Mike had read my application and that the fact I was fifteen was on it. To which, I was explained that Mike had to have overlooked it and sometimes he makes mistakes like that.

I closed my eyes and could no longer envision a big-boned, jolly fellow named Mike. I could see only a disgustingly fat, alcoholic asshole that was eating beef sticks in his underwear and didn't know how to read.

"I'm sorry about this, Ryan. Maybe in a couple of months when you turn sixteen you can come back and we can see if we have something for you," the other manager said as tears welled up in my eyes.

I pointed to my work shirt and started my puberty-voice stuttering again, saying I didn't have another shirt with me to change into.

"That's okay. You can keep the shirts. Free advertising, right?" he said as he stood up and indicated for me to follow him out of the office.

I stumbled out in a daze. I tried to keep it together. The manager walked away and I tried to remember where I had seen a payphone.

A waitress popped up in front of me. "Hey there," she boisterously said. "I'm Mandy. Do you want me to show you around?"

I tried to speak as low as I could to show that I wasn't about to start sobbing. "No thanks, Mandy. I am only fifteen. I guess I can't work here," I said and saw the manager from the corner of my eye. He was telling the waiter with the braces to be the dishwasher tonight. His eyes found mine and shot me a look that wanted my rotten, filthy guts to burn eternally in hell.

I looked back at Mandy as she looked at me like she was watching a dog being put to sleep.

"Oh, that's too bad. They should really ask that information on the applications before they hire people," she brilliantly reasoned.

I agreed and asked if she knew where a payphone was. She pointed me in the right direction. I walked over to it, feeling tears build up uncontrollably in my eyes. I lifted the phone to call my mom to pick me up. I reached in my pocket and found only two dimes.

No!

Crap.

I walked back over to Mandy, who was talking to another waitress and didn't seem to see—or care—that I was standing there. When she finally looked at me, I asked if I could borrow a nickel. She said she probably wouldn't get it back since I wouldn't be working there, and then she laughed, said she was just kidding, and gave me one.

When I got back to the phone, a fat cowboy was on it. I stared at him and tried not to look around the restaurant because the sheer absurdity of his cowboy outfit was the only thing keeping me from crying. His boots had spurs on them! The Rio Grand Steakhouse was in the middle of a strip mall of stores in suburbia. Where the hell did this guy come from, and what did he do for a living?

He hung up the phone, and I put my money in and dialed home. Busy. Tears started falling from my eyes now. My mom was probably on the phone with the other relatives, telling them all I'm at my first day of work. *Uh huh, his grandfather is very proud of him indeed. He'll probably be too pooped during the week to mow the lawn three times. Ha, ha, ha.*

I hung up the phone, walked out into the rain, and headed home.

The Rio Grand Steakhouse lost the most enthusiastic dishwasher they could ever hope to have that day. On the other hand, they got over an hour's worth of free advertising to people driving home and seeing a fifteen-year-old boy walking along the road, wearing a red shirt with bright yellow letters on the back that read: "Rio, Rio Good."

About the Author:

While slowly pursuing a teaching degree, Ryan Bennett has found himself stuck in the draining void of the restaurant industry. In his free time, when he's not discussing feminism with his wife Lindsay, or chasing his two dogs and two cats around the house, his intense introspection and determination for a creative outlet have resulted into writing his first novel.

He's currently in the midst of searching for a publisher and does not in any way shape or form agree with the comedy, purpose, or ideas presented by popular college prop comic Carrot Top.

HEMINGWAY AT THE RITZ
©2006 by Lou Dischler

Ernest Hemingway was staying at my hotel in Montare. The town was a medieval village in the south of France, maybe two dozen streets in all, and the Ritz was the only hotel in town. One afternoon I was ensconced in a comfortable chair in the lobby, idly looking out the cracked plate glass window. A cab pulled up outside and Hemingway emerged from the passenger door, saying something to the driver. After the cab drove off, he wrote in a small notebook, looked in both directions, and marched off down the street.

My business in the village was finished. Having the remainder of the day with nothing to do, I had a sudden urge to follow him. In a grocery two blocks away, I stood behind a wooden bin, pretending to examine cucumbers and plantains as Ernest spoke in French to a man in a black leather jacket. I had to lean forward to understand their words, because they spoke so quietly, and because my French had a few holes in it.

"Now you see," Ernest said, "I've bagged the samples, but getting them there is a problem." He picked up a fruit, frowning. His voice was muffled but I could still make it out: "These are hard plutoniums."

"Yes," the other man said, "they are very hard."

Disturbed by this conversation, so unlike the Hemingway I knew from *Old Man and the Sea*, I replaced a long cucumber in the bin and quickly left the grocery. Ernest must have seen me as I closed the door, because he nudged the other fellow, nodding in my direction. I looked away. Did they think I was spying? They had no reason to think that, did they? I had every right to buy fruit if I wanted to, though I now regretted that I hadn't.

As I walked away, I felt their eyes on me, boring into my back. Unnerved, I began to run, and immediately stumbled on a dislodged cobblestone, falling in the street. Cursing the French authorities for their haphazard maintenance, I stood, dusting myself off. Then I put one foot in front of the other, with my hands partially extended in front of me, for I no longer trusted this foreign soil to support me. Even though I was in excellent physical condition, I was breathing hard by the time I reached the hotel. Something was surely wrong. Going up the stairs, I used both hands on the railing. At the first landing, I felt my forehead. It was cool, almost cold. This was, I remembered, a sure sign of cholera.

In my room on the third floor, I locked the door. In the tiny bath, I dug through my toiletries bag, scattering small items on the countertop, finally finding the orange bottle of antibiotics. I swallowed four of the tablets, then another four from a blue bottle, washing them down with brandy. I didn't dare drink the hotel water—no telling what vile pathogens lurked in that milky fluid! I breathed deeply, wishing I were breathing bottled air instead. Wholesome American air, free of foreign impurities.

A little later, I had the phone in my hand when I heard the door of the room next to mine. Who was staying there I didn't know. I'm not usually the nosy type, but on an impulse, I hung up, placed a water glass flat on the adjoining wall, and put my ear to it. At first all I could hear was a muffled sound, someone talking, but underwater. I moved the glass around on the wall until all at once I recognized the voice. Hemingway!

"...four samples will go out in two days, six in five days, and more if you need them," he said in English. "You know how to reach me." There was silence for a moment as though the other person was saying something, and oh, how I wanted to know what it was! I wished I knew about tapping phones and so forth, but that wasn't my expertise. "A funny thing," Ernest continued, "a little man at the hotel was snooping around...no, it's probably nothing...well, you think? That seems a bit extreme...no, there's no room in the car, so I suppose I'll have to think of something. Perhaps I... yes, thank you. *Au revoir,*"

That seems a bit extreme. What on earth were they planning?

I realized that for a famous author like Hemingway, murder was just another thing to write about. Grist for the creative mill. And it occurred to me that he had even murdered himself many years before. But that couldn't be right, for here he was, secretly alive.

That worried me, for what might a man do to keep such a secret!

I stepped back and, butterfingers that I am, the glass slipped from my fingers. It struck the base of sculpture I'd found in Toulouse and rolled across the wooden floor, making an awful clatter. My god! I remained where I was, perfectly rigid. Silence in the next room, then the sounds of movement. Finally, I heard the door open and close. Sweat dripped from my armpits, making loud splats. Perhaps I only imagined they were loud, but I squeezed my arms against my body anyway, trying not to sweat, not even to breathe.

And then...a knock!

A single rap, then three more. Not loud, but not soft, either. I stood there, still as a statue, holding my breath. I could sense him out there, his hand touching the knob. I prayed that I had locked it. I did, didn't I? My chest was burning now. God, I was dying for air! At long last, he went away—I heard his feet on the stairs, the steps creaking. Breathing heavily, almost gasping, I moved over to the window. There he was, striding down the street. He turned suddenly, and I dropped to the floor. Did he see me? I prayed that he hadn't. Then it occurred to me—why shouldn't I look out the window? I had every right to do so! I was a guest of the Ritz, just like him.

I stood, angry with myself. Glowing spots scattered across my vision. Was I passing out? I sat on the edge of the bed and counted to fifty. The spots turned red, then black, then vanished. When I looked again, through a crack in the shutters this time, he was gone. I waited a few minutes, slipped a jacket over my damp shirt and went out into the hall. It took only a moment with a credit card to unlock the antique door, and soon I was rifling through his things, most of which were still in an enormous canvas suitcase— the kind with four wheels on the bottom, since it was too heavy to lift.

I was a man determined to preserve myself!

In the state I was in, I admit I lost my cool, and soon Hemingway's possessions were strewn about. There were many suspicious items—women's socks, dozens of them in zip-lock bags. Hemingway didn't wear socks, did he? Even more suspicious: there was no typewriter, no novel in progress.

With a growing unease, I turned over the case and dumped the remaining contents on the floor. On my knees, I tossed items about. I found nothing that could kill me, although doubtlessly, he was purchasing a weapon at that very moment. I imagined him returning with a Walter PPK, silencer attached, pointing it at my head, a brief puff of smoke, and then...nothing but a dark river, a boatman, and a dog. Or perhaps he would return with a long, serrated knife, force me into my room, and gut me there, my terrible screams muffled by duct tape.

Those scenarios seemed perfectly rational. That was when I found his notebook. Aha! So, he *was* still writing! I pocketed it without opening it, for I was suddenly feeling dizzy again. I lay on his bed, just for a moment, just to get my breath. It seemed more comfortable than my own bed, softer. And it seemed I had just closed my eyes when I heard a click. I jerked up. Ernest was there, closing the door, with a slight smile that did little to soften the murderous intent on his white, whiskered face.

"What are you doing in here?" he said.

"What are *you* doing in here?" I replied, doing my best to sound offended.

He looked at me hard, then looked at his suitcase, which was upended amidst a great pile of clothes. "You've made quite a mess of my room," he observed in heavily accented English. A phony accent, to be sure.

"But this is *my* room!" I stood and took a step towards him. "I've called the police, you should know that. With all this mess, I thought I'd been robbed."

His smile disappeared. "What is it you want from me?"

"From you?" I looked around, pretending confusion. "Oh, perhaps I did make..."

I trailed off, because he had his hand inside his coat—a lightweight tartan jacket, very touristy—and I was sure the lump I saw there was a revolver, chambered with an exploding round with my name on it: *Lenny Schwartz.*

The revolver was now in his hand, its silver muzzle pointing in my direction!

I considered jumping over the bed and hurling myself out the window, but I remembered it was three floors down, with hard cobblestones below. I had already experienced one collision with them and was reluctant to have another. When he unscrewed the muzzle, I saw I was mistaken. It was a silver flask, not a gun. He took a swig, licked his lips, then walked towards me, unsteadily, stopping very close. I could smell the brandy on his breath. Hemingway had always been a heavy drinker.

"These things happen," he said finally. "I've woken in the wrong room before."

He made a motion towards me with the flask, so I took it. With brandy, there are no pathogens, nothing to worry about, which is why I drank it almost exclusively. I took a long pull, thinking it particularly good—peach with a hint of...something I couldn't identify. Mangoes? Turnips? Only as I handed it back to him did I notice the bitter aftertaste. He didn't take the flask; he turned from me and began tidying up the mess I'd made. I tried to say something, but my vocal cords seemed rusty. I sipped more brandy, hoping to loosen them.

The early stages of a bacterial infestation, I was now convinced.

I sat on an overstuffed chair, listening to his lies as he repacked his items. He said he was a salesman for a sock manufacturer, on a working holiday. He glared at me when I laughed, yet it was such a pitiable fiction to come from a renowned novelist. I told him I was an art dealer and I too was on a working holiday, which wasn't fiction, but the truth. I finished the brandy, and soon enough found myself on the floor. Why was I lying there, unable to rise? Perhaps it was the cholera?

I saw Ernest pick up the heavy, black handset and speak into it. What he said I couldn't make out, because it sounded so far away.

So far

far

away.

And soon, I couldn't see or hear anything at all.

I woke in my own room, dressed as I'd been before, lying above the covers. It was dark out. I no longer felt choleric, but I swallowed a handful of antibiotics just to be safe: four tablets from my orange bottle, then another four from the blue, washing them down with a mouthful of brandy.

Hemingway's purpose was more mysterious than ever, for had he wanted to kill me, he could easily have done so. I was up half the night, listening with the glass, but nothing now, no sound at all. The next morning, as I was checking out, I asked the girl at the desk about him. She raised her eyebrows.

"Hemingway," I said, "the man in the room next to me, with the snow-white beard. Earnest Hemingway."

"Oh...you mean *Monsieur* Hennessey." She turned the ledger around and pointed to his entry: *E. Hennessey, Kansas City, Kansas.* I laughed as his *nom de plume* was so ludicrously transparent.

"Is anything wrong, *Monsieur*?"

"No, no, nothing's wrong."

Halfway across the Atlantic, feeling pressure in my ears, I put my hand in my jacket for a stick of gum and found his notebook. I stared at the battered leather cover for some time, wondering if I'd find notes for a new novel in it. Placed in the south of France, with myself as a minor character...or perhaps even the protagonist! But no, nothing of the sort. It was jammed with numbers and names, and many of the names were Russian. Not the notebook of an author. Not at all. But what? The answer came to me as we approached Miami International: Hemingway had become a smuggler! That explained his secrecy, and I felt an odd kinship to him, since I was in that business as well.

Going through customs, a grim-faced woman asked me to open my suitcase.

"No problemo," I said. When she started on my second suitcase without asking, I began coughing violently. That had always worked before, but this woman was not so easily distracted.

"What do we have here?" she asked, finding a stylized Greek bronze of a Trojan horse buried deep in my dirty underwear.

"It's a reproduction. I have paperwork for it somewhere, if you need to see it." It seemed unlikely she'd realized it was stolen, since it was just a minor piece from a private collection. But she didn't answer. She was busy examining it with her latex-gloved hands. Finally, she popped it free of the marble base and held it up, looking into the hole beneath the horse's chest, where the mounting pin had been.

"What's in here?"

"What's in where?" I said, trying to see what she was looking at.

"I'm going to have to ask you to stand against the wall," she said, cocking her head towards a burly man in uniform, "with that officer."

The last thing she did before she arrested me was to shake the horse. The little balls of plutonium that fell out made sharp raps on the sheet metal table. You can imagine how I felt when they told me! Smuggling plutonium is one of the worst things you can do, short of actually using it. It's such an awful thing that the government didn't want to prosecute, because they didn't want the public to know how often this sort of thing happened. Actually, they didn't say it was plutonium, they didn't even mention the balls, but I figured out that much. The little book of names turned out to be my salvation. They were so excited by the names in there that they decided to release me. All of those names belonged to terrorists. True, they didn't say that either, but some things didn't need saying. Hemingway was now playing one dangerous game. He should have stuck with the writing!

The government agents told me not to do any more smuggling. Not that they cared, really.

"We don't care about sculpture," one of them said.

"Then can I have my horse?"

The agent looked at a second agent and rolled his eyes. "Can you believe this guy?"

I took that to mean they were going to keep it.

It was a week after I'd returned from France, two days after the government let me go, that the bell over the door of my antique store tinkled. A man dressed in a bush jacket and khaki pants entered and began looking around. Every few moments, he would glance over at me. Do you know what Hemmingway looked like when he was younger? Heavy jaw, black mustache, khaki clothes? Unmistakable.

"May I help you?" I said from behind the counter.

He lifted his Sun-Also-Rises head and sauntered over to me. "Yes," he said, "perhaps you can. I'm looking for something for my girlfriend."

I closed the drawer with my pistol in it and put my hands flat on the oak countertop, friendly like. He was pretending not to recognize me, so I would play his game...for a time. "Anything in particular?"

"Well, she likes vases, sculpture, stuff like that."

"Stuff like that," I repeated. On the surface, Hemingway had a simple way of speaking, but between the words was quicksand!

He spent ten or fifteen minutes looking at the vases I showed him. I had some fine English and Chinese pieces, Victorian and Ming, which he examined with pretended indifference. "Well," I said finally, "I've got a few bronzes that might interest her."

"Okay. Let's have a look."

I walked him through my collection. He seemed unimpressed by my Greek gods and water nymphs. Uninterested in Roman senators and French nobility. "Anything in *particular?*" I asked, wondering when he would get to it.

"She likes to ride, so she might like a horse."

Might like a horse! Oh, now he was playing me! Okay, Hemingway, giddyup, on with the game! I showed him an equestrian Stonewall Jackson, but he didn't want that. A couple of mustangs frolicking, he just turned up his nose, which was as I expected, for the third act was reaching its inevitable climax.

"How about a Greek horse?" I said evenly.

"Hey, now you're talking."

Oh, yes, now I was talking!

"Right this way, *Papa*," I said, feeling dizzy. When I got him to the counter, I yanked open that drawer and pulled out my .38, training it on him. "Looking for your stuff?" I shouted. "Your little balls?"

He spread his hands in pretended confusion. "My God, I don't know what—"

"You deny you are Earnest Hemingway? That you used me to smuggle plutonium in a Trojan horse?"

"Are you crazy?" he said, reaching into his jacket for his Walter PPK, which it turned out he'd forgotten to pack that morning. He did have a knife in there, but unfortunately for me it was only a penknife, and even more unfortunately, he had a wallet in that same inside pocket. Hemingway, creative liar that he was, told the cops he was reaching for his ID when I shot him in the stomach. When they told me, I laughed and laughed, it was just so mind-boggling! Yet, the joke was on me in the end, because the authorities bought his story, as they say, hook, line and sinker—that he was the son of the governor of Florida!

Can you believe it? Of course not! But they did, even with all my evidence. Which is why you see me here in Avon Park

Correctional, doing ten to fifteen. But you know the truth? The plain and simple truth is that I'm a hero. It's people like me, who keep their eyes open. Who see what's in front of their noses, who tell others about it. So, when people like you see Hemingway on the street...

Well, you'll know what to do.

About the author:

A former senior scientist with 58 US patents, Lou began writing in 2003. In 2004, he won the Hardegree prize for a memoir, Autobiography of an Innocent Man. He has completed seven novels to date, the latest inspired by his connections to the Kennedy assassination.

DREAMING OF DANNY
©2006 by Qing Yang

Mika trudged on her heels along the lake. Eight hours of dancing! No wonder her feet hurt. When she danced she felt no pain at all; it was only when she stopped that it was unbearable. But this was her first dance festival and she didn't want to miss a thing.

The far side of the lake was well lit, though the night was dark. Mika didn't mind the darkness; she just wanted to get to her campsite. She imagined lying in the sleeping bag so her feet could rest. The longer she walked, the more pain she felt. Why hadn't she noticed before that the road from the dance hall to the campsite was so long? Halfway there, she started limping. She felt silly, but couldn't laugh.

Suddenly, she tripped and cried out. Before she fell to the ground, strong hands caught her waist from behind.

"Are you okay?" a man's concerned voice asked.

"Fine...thanks." Mika was out of breath and a little embarrassed.

"Be careful. It's dark and there are lots of roots on the ground." He offered her his hand, "Hold on."

Mika couldn't see his face clearly, but she could tell he was a tall young man. His voice was quite deep and strangely familiar. Had they danced before?

"Where is your tent?"

Mika pointed to a huge, rectangular tent about thirty yards

away. "Behind the big one..."

The young man walked hand in hand with Mika to her tent.

"Thank you very much."

"You're welcome. Have a good night, ma'am." The young man turned away.

Ma'am? Only Danny called her that. Could it be...?

"Wait," Mika called out after him. "What's your name?"

"Danny." He disappeared into the darkness.

Danny? "Wait!" Mika ran after him, but he was already out of sight. She searched franticly, but there was no sign of him. Mika stood frozen in the dark and almost cried. "Let me find him tomorrow, please!"

How could she forget Danny and that day? She was so miserable when he showed up in her life. How long ago was that? Six months and 12 days. Mika was counting.

A year ago, her boyfriend of three years left her for her best friend. It was such a shock. She was away for a conference, and came back a day ahead of schedule and found them lying in bed together.

Could anybody imagine the pain she went through? Later, she imagined a girl falling down a steep valley. She saw herself hanging on rocks by the cliff, sliding inch by inch down the hollow. She wanted to pull herself up, but she wasn't strong enough. All she could do was sit in the corner of her apartment, fold herself into a ball, and watch that girl fall further and further down the valley.

A couple of weeks later, she went to seek professional help since she couldn't function on her own. She had to take an antidepressant in order to keep going. Six months after breaking up with her boyfriend, she was twenty pounds thinner. Many of her friends thought she looked ten years older. Her lovely smile and vitality were gone, disappeared into the thin air, replaced by frowns and sadness.

The only hope she had at the time was her dreams. A kind,

good-looking young man appeared in them repeatedly, offering her hope for the future.

One night she was on her way back from the weekly therapy session. Mika could never forget the scary sky.... It rained, sleeted, and snowed on her way to the therapy session. By the time she left, the road was covered by icy snow. The streets were empty; no cars in sight. It was so dark, Mika felt eerie. It was only half an hour drive to her apartment, but she hurried, forgetting that snow and ice driving requires patience and slow speeds.

She kept her right foot on the gas, until she saw a deer jumping cross the road. She slammed on the brakes and immediately her car spun out of control on the slippery road.

Panicked, she cried out, "No!"

The car made a one hundred and eighty degree turn then went off the road and down a steep hill.

"I'm going to die."

Mika remembered later that she wasn't scared, but actually a little relieved. She'd never thought about suicide before, but life wasn't important any more without her boyfriend. She didn't care one way or another about living or dying. She knew it was a terrible way to feel, but there was nothing she could do about it.

Mika saw trees at the bottom of the hill flying toward her. "Oh, God!" She inhaled and closed her eyes as the car slammed into a large pine.

Three days later, she woke up in a hospital. Everybody said she was lucky, that an angel must have been with her that night. Otherwise, she wouldn't have survived. She knew it was true. She had seen the angel: a young man in his early twenties. She remembered it as clearly as if happened yesterday.

As her car hit the tree, Mika felt her body smash into the steering wheel and shatter into pieces like glass. She'd never experience anything so painful. Luckily, her body quickly became numb.

Somehow, she managed to jump out of the car. To her astonishment and disbelief, she saw someone leaning lifelessly on the steering wheel inside her car. That someone was *her*. She wrestled with the mystery of it, but it was too strange and mystifying to think about. It seemed she had simply left her body as energy or a spirit would.

The front of the car started burning. Mika felt the urge to tell the girl in the car to get out, but she was voiceless. Franticly, she tried to open the door and pounded hard on it, but it made no difference. She felt like an invisible ghost.

She started to float. Glancing down as she went up, Mika saw a young man tumbling down the hill. He tried to open the badly jammed driver's door, but after a few tries, he dashed to the other side of the car. It was the same: he couldn't open it. He kicked the door a couple of times, but it was still no use.

Mika looked up. A dark tunnel with a bright light at the far end hovered right above her. The tunnel, especially the light, was fascinating. Mika felt the urge to go in. She turned around and looked down one more time, worried about the man who was trying to rescue the girl in the car.

The young man, appearing to know it would take too much time to open the door, decided to extinguish the fire first. He took his jacket off, swayed it high above his head, and patted it hard on the fire. Once, twice, three times.... He kept stamping on the fire.

Mika couldn't see his face clearly, but somehow knew he was very handsome. The way he moved was strong and elegant, like a dancer. She was drawn to him. She wanted to go back to help him. The light at the end of the tunnel, however, was powerful. It offered something unknown, something mysterious, but comforting and positive. It pulled her further into the tunnel.

"Come on, come on!" Mika heard the young man talking to himself. His voice was very deep, like a singer's. It seemed surprisingly familiar.

"Where have I heard his voice before?" Mika forced herself out of the tunnel. She wanted to see how the young man was doing.

His jacket caught fire and he threw it away. Bending to the ground, he gathered up slush with both hands and repeatedly threw it onto the car. To her amazement, the fire became smaller and eventually disappeared. Total darkness then covered the area.

Mika felt the warmth from the light at the end of the tunnel. She was compelled to move up again towards the light. It was warm and quiet in the tunnel; peaceful, calm, and comforting. Mika flew up effortlessly.

"Ma'am? Are you okay? Can you hear me?"

She heard the young man talking to her. Somehow, he had managed to open the door while Mika was engulfed by the warmth and light of the tunnel. Under the dim light shining from inside of the car, she saw a pry bar lying by the side of the door. She guessed he must have used it to get to her.

Ma'am? Nobody calls me ma'am. She smiled to herself, thinking he was too polite. She wanted him to call her Mika, but she knew he couldn't hear her.

"Hang on." The young man said firmly. "You'll be okay. Hang on." His voice was so kind, like he was talking to a dear friend.

Mika looked at the young man. His face was covered with ashes. She couldn't see much except his tall, straight nose and his large dark eyes. Those beautiful eyes instantaneously captivated her. They seemed oddly familiar. Mika was entranced by them, and she was now torn between the pulling power of going up and the urge of going back.

With strong hands, the young man gently took Mika by the waist and lifted her out of the driver's seat. "Hold on," he said to her face as he carried her in his arms. "Hold on," he repeated, marching up the hill. "You will be fine. You hear me? Just hold on."

His voice was so kind and concerned; Mika could feel his emotion. His arms were so comforting; she wanted to stay there and let him hold her.

"I have to go back!" Mika said to herself. "He is right. I have to live! I'm so young. There is a whole new life in front of me." Mika stared at the young man again. "He is such a nice guy. I have to meet him. I want to be with him. He must be the man in my dreams."

Mika struggled with the mysterious force above her and forced herself to move down, escaping the lure of comfortable feelings that inexplicable light offered. She had to use all her will power. "He is the one." She kept telling herself. "He is the one in my dreams. Don't miss the chance to be with this wonderful guy. Go, keep on going down."

She did it. She pulled herself out of the tunnel and flew back to Earth, to her own body, and in his arms. The last thing she remembered was his beautiful, concerned eyes. Suddenly, she felt excruciating pain all over her body again and lost consciousness.

Later, in the hospital, when she managed to speak, she told the doctors of her experience. They looked at each other, then one of them spoke. "You had a near death experience. Some people claim they are real, but most people believe they are just hallucinations or dreams."

"But...it can't be a dream. It was so real!"

The doctor nodded sympathetically. "It's possible. It's...a miracle that you are still alive, considering how bad the accident was." The doctor didn't tell her she had died then; the man who had rescued her told the paramedics he couldn't feel her pulse for several minutes. But miraculously and unaccountably she'd returned to life.

"It was a young man," one young nurse said in a quiet voice, "who rescued you."

"Who is he? What's his name?" Mika asked anxiously.

"Uh...Danny. That's all I know. He's tall and..." the nurse smiled mischievously, "...good looking, I believe. His face was covered with ashes, but, you know, sometimes you can still tell...from the eyes or the way he walks and talks...you know what I mean."

Mika knew exactly what she was talking about. She felt the same way. She remembered his big, dark, piercing eyes. They were so compelling, magnetic. She recalled being drawn to them.

After the accident, Mika's life was immensely changed. She became a totally different person. Her friends could hardly recognize her. She changed from inside and out. She used to be shy and quiet, especially after she broke up with her boyfriend. She had never talked much or showed emotions too openly. She hadn't even allowed herself to wear anything other than blue, green, or gray.

Now she owned several bright colored skirts and dresses. She even started to wear earrings and necklaces. She started taking dance lessons and soon became, as she put it: a dancing fanatic; or as her friends put it: a dance fairy. More importantly and profoundly, her spirit was exceedingly high. She felt so alive and couldn't believe that she had doubted living before. Life seemed so precious to her now and she didn't want to waste a minute.

Only one thing, though, bothered her. She wasn't able to find out who the young man was and how he had saved her. All she knew was his name. Danny. Nowadays, whenever she heard the name, she would turn and study whoever was being called Danny.

She wanted so much to find the young man who not only saved her that night, but also changed her life forever. She wanted to thank him for giving her a second chance in life. She wanted to thank him for being so brave and kind. She wanted to tell him that she fell in love with him in his arms that night.

His face, mostly covered with ashes except his dark piercing eyes, appeared in her dreams from time to time. Every time she had such dreams, she woke up crying and smiling at the same time. She loved seeing him in her dreams, but how she wished it were real! How she longed to see him in flesh and blood! How she yearned to talk to him face to face! And how she craved to dance with him hand in hand! That would be a dream come true to her.

Well, tomorrow, her dream of Danny might finally come true. With teardrops still at the corner of her eyes, a slight, soft smile appeared on her lips as she fell asleep.

About the Author:

Qing Yang, Ph.D. resides in Chapel Hill, North Carolina, USA. Her recent foray into creative writing has proven an exciting digression from her lengthy portfolio of scientific publications. Graduate work in Molecular Biology brought her to the United States from her native China.

One of several short stories, "White Lily of Easter", written through her multicultural lens, tells an inspirational story of a small white flower that represented hope for many WWII POWs and then adds love and death together to create a heartbreaking saga. It has won an Honorable Mention in the "Beauty of Aging Unveiled Competition", an Honorable Mention in the "Annual Hidden Talents Short Story Contest", and has been published in *Tall Tales and Short Stories* (Tall Tales press Book Publishing Inc.)

Dreaming of Danny reflects her own struggles and feelings in life and her hope for finding the love she has been searching for. Besides writing, her hobbies include dancing, flying, hiking, traveling, skydiving, scuba diving, music and art.

ROMEO AND SIERRA'S LAST MISSION
©2006 by Bill Westhead

Furious winds flung the two-seater Piper Comanche ski plane about the inky black sky as the pilot, code-named Romeo, fought to maintain altitude. One hundred feet below lay the raging waters of the Bering Straits, where giant waves hurled large chunks of ice skywards, like ack-ack fire, constantly threatening to cripple the small aircraft. The only light in the cockpit came from the iridescent glow of the instrument panel. His navigator, known in the service as Sierra, sat alongside, strapped tightly into his well-padded seat, his mouth dry and his mittened fingers beating a silent tattoo on the map case.

The coldness of the cabin penetrated their fur-lined flying suits and—not for the first time—Sierra wondered why they had volunteered for this mission. He and Romeo were getting too old for this game, but neither had been able to resist one last shot at the old adversary whose military continued to menace several smaller countries. If this strike, the first of many, proved successful, the enemy would be forced to recall its troops to guard vital home installations, thus curtailing the spread of their unwanted ideology....

Crossing the Straits at this point should, Sierra calculated, have taken about an hour, but after seventy minutes there was still no sight of land. He could only guess how far south they had been driven by the gale.

"I don't know where the hell we are," Sierra shouted. "If you can climb a bit higher, I may be able to find a landmark."

"Daren't do that," Romeo shouted back. "Above a hundred feet we'll be picked up by their damned coastal radar and they'll scramble their fighters. If that happens, we're in even worse trouble."

Sierra nodded. It seemed they were damned if they did and damned if they didn't. He would just have to trust to luck that they were heading toward the coast and not running parallel with it. He longed for a cigarette but the faint odor of gasoline from the extra tanks behind them stopped him. It also reminded him that their flight time was limited: sufficient fuel to get to their destination and back, but with little to spare.

He glanced behind at the three backpacks. The large one contained a hundred pounds of plastic high explosive and fuses, while the other two held sleeping bags, a small 2-man tent, ten loaded magazines, and several packages of iron rations in case of emergencies. Their full-weather whites, two AK-47 rifles fitted with silencers, and two pairs of skis with their poles rested on top.

For a moment, he let his mind drift back to the first mission he and Romeo had been assigned: Cuba, more than thirteen years ago. Both had been sent to keep watch and report on the build up of missiles in that island nation. It would be nice to be back in Cuba, he thought. But that could never be. All the missiles had been withdrawn years ago and both he and Romeo had moved onward and upward in the organization.

He continued to peer ahead through the rain-slashed windshield. If they didn't sight land soon, they would not have sufficient fuel to make the return trip. His stomach tightened as he thought what that would mean. Suddenly, he spotted a line of breakers.

"Port," he yelled in Romeo's ear, pointing at the line of white foam.

The buffeting increased as the Piper turned across the howling winds. With the 180-horsepower engine running smoothly, they approached the coast. Now the lights of a small town appeared below and Romeo aimed for a narrow valley that opened up between the snow-covered mountains ahead. The turbulence decreased as they flew into the pass. For another half hour the plane zigzagged through the mountain chain, never climbing higher than the surrounding peaks. Finally, the mountains gave way to the flat, open interior and the small aircraft bucked as the pilot turned north directly into the storm.

"Reckon another forty-five minutes to landing," Sierra shouted.

"Looks as though we'll make it," Romeo said. There was no hiding the relief in his voice.

At the appropriate time, Romeo cut the engine. Now there was only the swish of the wind as he gently lowered the nose towards the deceptively flat, snow-covered tundra. Within minutes they felt a shudder as the skis touched down. Then, without warning, the front ski struck an ice ridge and shattered. The nose tilted forward and the two-bladed propeller hit the frozen ground with a crunching sound. The two men were hurled forward and upward as the plane cart-wheeled onto its back. Shaken, but unhurt, they struggled out of their harnesses, forced the doors open, and jumped to the ground. Looking at the smashed propeller and crumpled port wing, both men saw the Comanche would never fly again. Their means of retreat was gone.

"I'm damned glad we brought emergency supplies," Sierra said, as they unloaded their backpacks, rifles, and skis.

Within minutes, they had donned their full-weather whites, making them almost invisible in the barren Arctic waste.

"Before we go any further," said Romeo, staring at the wreck "We'd better call HQ, tell them our problem, and ask them to send an aircraft to pick us up."

"You're right," Sierra said. "We've got eight-hour fuses. That should give us enough time to get back here and aboard before they blow."

Sierra climbed back in the shattered cockpit and cranked up the small portable radio. Over the crackling airwaves he briefly explained their situation and plan of escape.

There was a long pause at the other end before the officer answered. "If you're successful, they'll be waiting to intercept us on the return trip," he said. "We daren't risk an aircraft. You'll have to find another way."

Sierra started to argue but an emphatic click told him there was no one listening at the other end.

"The only other way is boat," Romeo said, leaning against the door. "Which means we've *got* to make the coast. Let's have a look at that map."

In the shelter of the damaged cockpit, they unfolded the map and, shading the flashlight, studied possible escape routes.

"This seems our best bet," Sierra said after several minutes. "We might be able to ski down the river to this point where it turns south, then cross-country to the other river, here, and straight to this inlet. If the map's right, that last stretch passes between two mountain ranges, so it should be reasonable going."

"It's a hell of a long way," Romeo said, as his partner used finger measurements to estimate the length of their proposed route.

"I reckon about two-hundred fifty miles," Sierra finally said. "Fortunately," he added, "most of it is uninhabited. The main danger will come from the air. Once we've blown the line they'll be searching for us."

"Well, you're the navigator so I'll have to trust you," Romeo said, then paused. "With any luck they'll only be able to search for us during the two or three hours of full daylight. How long do you think it'll take us?"

Sierra looked at the map again before answering. "I'd say eight days. That's about thirty-five miles a day plus a day for eventualities."

"We can cover more than that in a day," Romeo argued.

"We might, but we don't know what the going will be like, not to mention carrying fifty-pound backpacks and ten-pound rifles."

"Can't we bury the rifles and magazines?" Romeo said. "Save weight."

"How the hell do we find food if our rations run out, or protect ourselves against attack from man or animal? No, we take the rifles."

Romeo nodded.

"Anyway," Sierra added, "I'd rather hole up for an extra day and be sure than arrive late."

Finally, the two men agreed to ask HQ for a submarine to be in the inlet at midnight on the twenty-fifth. Sierra cranked up the radio again and waited. When the same officer answered, he outlined their alternative escape plan and gave the coordinates of their proposed rendezvous.

There was another long pause.

"I reckon the fool's sleeping," muttered Sierra as he waited.

"Has the ice started to break up?" the officer asked. "If not, we can't get a sub up there."

"Well you'd better damn well try," Sierra said. "If not, we're done for."

"We'll give it a shot. Roger and out." The radio went dead.

"Now that's settled, let's go," Romeo said, as he strapped on his skis and slid the straps of the explosives backpack onto his shoulders. "How far to the target?"

"Three miles," Sierra said, strapping on his skis and shouldering the two smaller packs, then added with a chuckle, "if my calculations are correct."

Despite the fact that both men were excellent cross-country skiers, the going proved harder than either had expected. Although their route ran parallel with the ice ridges, the wind, howling from the north, slashed at their partially covered faces. The straps of the packs soon began to dig into their shoulders.

It took just under an hour to reach the shelter of a shallow depression, where they could scan their target through high-powered, infrared binoculars. It was five o'clock in the morning. The unguarded pipeline, carrying thousands of gallons of crude oil to ports along the coast, lay less than a quarter mile away.

"We need to get on with it," Romeo said after a few minutes. "If we waste any more time we're going to be caught in daylight."

Leaving the depression, the two men crossed the intervening ground. Up close, the structure was impressive—the forty-eight-inch pipe, supported on large H-shaped frameworks sixty feet apart, zigzagged away in both directions as far as the eye could see.

"I hope the explosives we've got are powerful enough to damage this thing," Romeo said, gazing at the imposing structure. "I never realized it was this big."

"They'll work," Sierra said confidently. "*If* we get the stuff in the right place. Now come on. As you said, we haven't time to waste."

Removing their packs and unstrapping their skis, the two men clambered onto the cross beam of the first framework and wired explosives round both the pipe and its support. Then they moved to the next framework and repeated the procedure. As the sky began to lighten, ushering in another short day at the end of a long Arctic winter, all the explosives had been wired and the fuses set. Satisfied they had completed their mission, the two men re-shouldered their rifles and backpacks and, in twilight, skied alongside the pipeline.

At intervals, the silence of the early morning was shattered by rifle fire, as each man emptied two 30-round magazines of armor-piercing bullets into the pipe itself, causing trickles of crude oil to leak onto the tundra. Finally, deciding they could do no further damage, they made for the river.

Now the long ice ridges lay across their route, necessitating crab-like climbing up one side before skiing down the other. Negotiating this unforgiving terrain expended both time and energy. Warmed by the exercise, trickles of sweat began to pour down their bodies.

"We're going to have to slow down," Sierra said, thrusting his poles into the frozen surface and coming to a halt. "If we continue to sweat like this we'll suffer frost bite at best and a frozen death at worst when we stop."

By the time they reached the river, the Arctic day was spent and night was well advanced. But, even in the darkness, they could see that the ice had started to break up. Large slabs were piling up one on top of the other in the sluggish current. Their only course lay along the bank where more ice ridges and snow drifts, some twenty feet high, blocked their way. After two backbreaking hours they were forced to rest, squatting in the shelter of a large drift.

"We can't stay here," Sierra said, after a few minutes. "If we do, we'll freeze to death and we're still much too close to the pipeline."

Wearily, they staggered to their feet, the ultimate fear of capture coupled with the dropping temperature giving them the extra strength they needed to keep moving. Finally, after three hours fighting both the terrain and the elements, they were too exhausted to go any further. Halting at the foot of yet another high snow bank, they scooped out an area and pitched their stark white, two-man tent. In the darkness, each ate one of his precious iron ration packages, munching on pre-cooked sausage and rice, followed by a pemmican biscuit and a chocolate bar. They washed the meal down with semi-melted snow, its iciness stinging their parched throats. Near collapse, they crawled into their sleeping bags and immediately dropped off into a dreamless sleep.

When they woke, the day was almost over and the silvery sky already darkening. Although they had heard nothing, a glance at their watches told them the pipeline must have blown. Search parties would now be scouring the area. Wasting no time, each breakfasted on another iron ration package and semi-melted snow. Stuffing their sleeping bags in their backpacks with the neatly folded tent, they set out on another punishing trek through the Arctic darkness.

As they reached the point where the river turned south, daylight began to penetrate the heavy overcast. By now, the gale had blown itself out, replaced with gently falling snow.

"Just what we need," Romeo said, a smile crossing his face as he watched snowflakes land with airy puffs on his outstretched arm. "It won't hinder us, but it will keep their search planes grounded. It'll also cover our ski tracks. Couldn't be better if we had ordered it ourselves."

"Luck sometimes favors silly people," Sierra said, as they climbed into their sleeping bags. "Let's hope it keeps up while we head for the second river."

Twilight was settling over the wilderness as they left the river behind, their confidence restored. Sierra led, his companion following in his tracks. Navigating with the river to guide them had been easy, but now striking out across country, they would have to rely on their compass. An hour later, Sierra stopped and began juggling the compass from position to position.

Unconcerned and thankful for the rest, Romeo removed his backpack and squatted down. *I wish I was twenty years younger*, he thought, as he rubbed his cramping thighs.

"This damn thing's not working properly," Sierra muttered. "The needle points in any direction it wants." Again, he juggled the compass before turning to Romeo. "We can't rely on this," he continued. "Traveling by night, we'll have to hope we can pick a point to the left of the North Star until we come in sight of that pass through the mountains. We may also be able to check our position by the sun even if we can't see it. If we keep the sunrise behind us and the sunset ahead, we'll be traveling in the right direction."

"I hope you know what you're doing," Romeo said, continuing to rub his thighs. "Frankly, in this weather, 1 can't tell much difference between day and night. As for seeing the North Star!" He stopped, knowing they had to pull together if they hoped to be rescued. The escape route that seemed so straightforward on the map was proving otherwise in reality.

Crossing from the first river to the second proved no easier than the initial trek. In addition to the compass problem and only rare glimpses of the stars, ice ridges continued to crisscross the whole area while, here and there, chasms and crevasses appeared, causing them to ski at right angles to their line of march, sometimes several miles, until they could find a safe place to cross. They would have felt safer tied together, but their emergency supplies did not include a rope.

While swallowing snow helped to relieve their dry mouths, the effect was short lived. They believed their strenuous schedule was the cause of their constant thirst, unaware they were suffering the onset of dehydration. In a trance-like state they skied on, hours sliding by like minutes, their minds avoiding the present and wandering to thoughts of home and family. Each day, they grew a little weaker. Even the simple task of erecting their tent became a monumental effort. They forced themselves to eat, although by now they were sick of the taste of sausage, rice, pemmican, and chocolate. Only the experience gained from years of rigorous training and working together, kept them going.

When they reached the second river, six precious days had elapsed since the crash and they estimated they still had seventy miles to go to the rendezvous. Despite removing their boots and mittens and rubbing their feet and hands with snow every time they stopped, the ends of their fingers and toes were showing signs of severe frost bite. Food was also getting scarce, each man having but three iron ration packages left.

"They're going to have to last us for at least another two days," Sierra said, rubbing his left foot before crawling into his sleeping bag, "unless we want to eat raw meat." He paused before adding, "Thank God we allowed for an extra day."

Too exhausted to speak, Romeo nodded his agreement.

As the short day faded into night they forced themselves to consume one each of their precious food packs before starting out. They skied in Indian file with Romeo leading. For the first time, the gods seemed to smile on them. The snow was pristine, the ground level, and only the occasional snowdrift barred their way. In a hypnotic rhythm, they pushed on until their path was blocked by a large drift. About to take their first steps, they heard the distant beating of helicopter blades. The sound increased as the aircraft approached rapidly from the north, its large searchlight sweeping the ground ahead. Instinctively, both men cowered in the lee of the drift, clutching their rifles, hardly daring to breathe. After all they had suffered, it seemed ironic they should be captured so close to rescue. Within a few minutes the helicopter arced in over them at no more than a hundred feet, the light beam passing back and forth within a few feet of where they crouched.

"If he turns, we're spotted," Romeo whispered, as though any sound would give their position away. "Why don't we try and shoot him down?"

"He'll be on his radio at the first shot," Sierra said. "Our best hope is that he won't spot us."

The two men huddled closer to the shelter of the drift, hearts pounding and bellies churning as they listened to the noise rising and falling as the helicopter crisscrossed the area with military precision. After a few minutes, which seemed like hours, the clacking of the blades began to fade. Romeo slowly raised his head and turned in the direction of the receding sound. Some half mile away, he saw the searchlight continuing to flash across the snow.

"He's missed us," he said, tapping Sierra on the shoulder. "Damn, that was close. Don't know how he missed our ski tracks."

"Perhaps he didn't, but was fooled by seeing only one set," Sierra said, gulping in the ice laden air. "Still, we'd better wait until he's completely out of sight. If he returns and we are caught in the open..." There was no need for him to complete the sentence.

For two vital hours the men continued to crouch in the lee of the snowdrift, their bodies growing colder as each moment passed. Their steps, when they finally started up the drift, were clumsy and uncoordinated, the biting cold penetrating every muscle in their emaciated bodies. Pain shot through their arms and legs at each step.

Finally, they reached the crest. Warmed by the climb, they paused, gasping for air, then, thankfully, started down the other side. Slowly the pain subsided and within the half-hour they were back in their trance, gliding like automatons over the powdery snow.

As the sky lightened in the east they struggled to pitch their tent for what both prayed would be the last time. Inside, they eyed the remaining ration packs; loathe to eat the contents, yet knowing they needed the stamina for the final push to the inlet.

The night was clear when they woke. In the enveloping silence they stood and surveyed the vast emptiness that lay about them. Each felt as if he was the last human to inhabit the Earth. After a few minutes, they ate the last of their rations. Gambling on the success of their escape, they buried all but one of their spare magazines, lightening their loads by almost ten pounds. Abandoning the tent would save another fifteen pounds, but they decided against such drastic action. Buoyed by the thought that this would be the last leg of their ordeal, they shouldered their rifles and backpacks. But the lighter packs seemed to make little difference to their aching backs as they doggedly skied towards the rendezvous.

Late on the twenty-fifth the two exhausted men collapsed on the banks of the inlet. Wrapped in their sleeping bags, they gazed out across the water, its surface strewn with chunks of ice, and waited in hope that a submarine would surface somewhere out in the bay.

"Assuming they make it, I guess we've about three hours to wait," Sierra said, glancing at his watch.

Midnight came and went. One o'clock passed, then two. Their hopes rapidly fading, Sierra and Romeo began to think of their next move. Although both spoke the language fluently, they did so with sufficient accent to arouse suspicion among the natives. They might pass for hunters for a time, but even so, they still faced the problem of crossing the Bering Straits.

"We'll just have to take it one day at a time," Romeo said, drawing a snow-filled breath, holding it deep in his lungs before letting it out slowly. "I know it's a wild idea but if we follow this inlet we might find a boat."

Sierra stared at him. "You saw what the Straits were like from the air," he said. "How the hell do you think the two of us could cross in a boat? We'd be sunk in no time. I reckon if they don't come, we've no alternative but to surrender. At best we'll spend the rest of our lives in one of their military prisons. At worst we'll be shot. Still, those possibilities seem preferable to freezing to death here or," he added, "drowning in the Straits."

He had just finished speaking when the bay seemed to erupt, and up though the floes appeared a conning tower, followed rapidly by the outline of a submarine. Too exhausted to cheer, the two men scrambled to their feet and watched with tears in their eyes as a rubber boat was launched over the side. Within minutes they were clambering down the inside of the conning tower as fast as their frozen limbs allowed. Once everyone was safely aboard, the skipper gave the order to dive. A harsh grinding sound of ice against metal could be heard as the submarine started to descend.

"Welcome, Comrade Seriyev," Captain Kosloff said, turning from the periscope to offer his hand to Sierra. "And you too, Comrade Rodia," he added turning to Romeo.

Seven days later, the submarine reached its homeport of Petropavlovsk and the two agents were flown to Moscow. Here they learned of the success of their mission. In a little over two weeks, three divisions of enemy troops had been airlifted from Germany and were now patrolling the entire 840 miles of the Alaskan pipeline.

About the author:

Born in Clitheroe, England, and educated at Rossall School, Bill Westhead graduated from Leeds University with an honors degree in Textile Engineering. He is the fourth generation of his family to work in the textile industry.

After service in the British Army, he worked in the synthetic fiber industry in Wales, England and Northern Ireland. In 1973 he and his family emigrated to Waycross, Georgia where as Vice President/Company Director, he was primarily responsible for the design and development of heavy industrial fabrics for use in the manufacture of paper.

A member of Southeastern Writers Association and Coastal Writers Group he has published four historical novels, 'Once in

Old Frederica Town' (1993), 'Clogs' (1999), Confederate Gold' (2002) and 'The Mill', a sequel to 'Clogs' (2005). All four novels continue to be available on Amazon.com. He is also the author of several short stories published in 'Cricket', 'Animal Tales' and 'Chicken Soup for the Dog Lover's Soul' as well as non-fiction articles in 'Crafts 'n Things' and a number of trade magazines.

Currently he is working on his fifth novel while, at the same time, writing a monthly theater column 'Footlights' for the Waycross Journal Herald.

When not writing, he divides his time between working on his Bonsai collection and the Waycross Area Community Theatre where, over a number of years, he has undertaken every aspect of local theater from acting and directing to sweeping out the house.

www.ingramcontent.com/pod-product-compliance
Lightning Source LLC
Chambersburg PA
CBHW051250170626
46809CB00004B/1581